LARRY FRANCIS

An Anthropology of Anonymity

Time & Place Prize Publishing
Chicago

Copyright © 2018 by Larry Francis

Author photo Copyright © 2015 by E.E.C.

Text set in Palatino Linotype

A Time & Place Prize Publication
Chicago

ISBN — 13: 978-0-69-291167-9

For everyone who has died or will die,

and for my sister, Lee

An Anthropology of
Anonymity

Ama nesciri

IMMORTALITY

A CAVE

The slow silty current of the Vézère flows southwest, meandering past broad-shouldered willows and fragrant meadows, before joining the muddy Dordogne at Limeuil. A few miles upstream from this meeting of the waters, near an easy bend in the river, at the small village of Les Eyzies, tower the deeply weathered, karst-tipped cliffs of the Périgord Noir. These improbable precipices pop up without warning, suddenly soaring from the valley floor, inviting and imposing, but most of all, enchanting; as if molded by a million childhood imaginations. From a distance the towering bluffs look artificial, misplaced, shaped by hand, not by time, a mixture of child's clay and soil, play and toil. And the closer one gets to these high pocked walls, via twist and turn of road or river, the more the movie-set outcrops beckon. A disarming physiognomy appears. The rock faces coalesce preternaturally as both soft and severe. It is an incongruous mixture, an appealing simulation. One feels a staggering, almost palpable, attraction, a deep-seated visual siren's song emanating from the ancient stone. The attraction increases the closer you get; excitement builds. And then you arrive near enough to descry doorways stippled into the crags, holes in the ridges, passageways into the soaring black and tan mysteries. The timeless escarpments and rolling hills in this otherwise modest valley of rural France are dotted with caverns, dozens and dozens of caverns. These are the famous Cro-Magnon caves of our ancestors, the Paleolithic grottos of the Dordogne.

For tens of thousands of years man has taken refuge in this valley, within these cool narrow cavities, enticed by the felicitous confluence of protection and bounty, rock and river, sheltered by the beguiling overhangs carved by time into the creamy limestone. And man has left his mark. He has bequeathed an extraordinary record of his presence. For within these honeycombed crags, tucked beneath the long projections—on the light surfaces lining the dark caverns—are paintings, manmade illustrations, hundreds and hundreds of representations: outlines of hands, depictions of animals, drawings of symbols and sketches of signs. These enigmatic markings represent the forever frozen thoughts of early man. This is the sacred art gallery of our ancestors. This is the language of human prehistory.

In the mid-nineteenth century amateur enthusiasts invaded the sleepy Vézère Valley documenting, cataloging, and sometimes, damaging the ancient artwork. Spelunkers explored the passageways; scientists expounded on the short, brutish lives of the primitive artists. Local residents inhabiting the galleries were forced out. The caverns were mapped. The ancient paintings were drawn, photographed and copied. Word spread. The curious arrived. Commerce followed. Tours began. In short order the valley became renowned, celebrated as the cradle of prehistoric man. And tourism exploded.

North of the alluring and busy drama of Les Eyzies, where the valley floor begins to flatten and the hills start to slump, one decorated cave awaited rediscovery. The cave will be called Lascaux.

On an early autumn day, not long after the start of the Second World War, across the Vézère from the town of Montignac, a French teenager by the name of Marcel Ravidat was hiking a hillside with his dog, Robot, when the dog disappeared beneath a bush. Robot had stumbled into the tiny mouth of a cave. A few days later Ravidat returned with a pick axe, a shovel and three friends. Together they enlarged the cavity and stepped back in time, tens of thousands of years back in time. What they saw amazed them. The cave overbrimmed with Upper Paleolithic paintings, room after illustrated room, nearly two thousand figures in all. Robot the dog had sniffed out the single greatest collection of prehistoric art heretofore known to man. By the end of the year—amid the exigencies of war—the French government had the cave site declared a national treasure.

Today the iconic paintings of Lascaux have become part of our collective patrimony and are so well known they require little description: images rendered in reds and yellows and blacks, paintings of large animals: equines, stags, cattle and bison, aurochs and felines. There is a bird and a bear, as well as a rhinoceros and the outline of a human. In a chamber dubbed the Hall of Bulls, one black bull spans seventeen feet. In another room named the Apse (*Abside* in French) every available surface, including the ceiling, is covered with countless entangled, overlapping, engraved drawings, like an LSD trip made manifest.

But it is not only the sheer number of images that sets Lascaux apart. It is the artistic skill on display. The paintings are alive. The aurochs in the Hall of Bulls appear to be in motion, a human first. And in one painting—the so-called *Crossed Bison*—the crossed hind legs create the illusion that one bison is closer to the viewer than the other, a primitive form of perspective, another artistic first for our species.

The seventeen-thousand-year-old parietal art these four teenaged Frenchmen rediscovered by lamplight is acclaimed now, deservedly, reprinted time and time again in anthropology, history and art books read and studied around the world. Lascaux, the jewel of the Vézère Valley, the adorable infant cooing in the cradle of prehistory, is synonymous with incipient human creativity and the beginnings of art.

Yes, to be sure, the artwork is famous, but what about the artists? Who were they? Who left us this marvelous treasure? And why?

The answer unfortunately is that we do not know who they were, the ancient people who populated these gentle hillsides. Oh, we give them names. We call them Aurignacian or Tayacian based on tool usage or Périgordian denoting location. Even the clownish-sounding Cro-Magnon persists despite lacking taxonomic standing. (For the pedantic, the current agreed-upon name among scientists is European early modern humans or EEMH.) But the truth is we do not know, nor will we ever know, who these people were. Anthropologists suspect Neanderthals (*Homo neanderthalensis*) occupied the relatively comfortable valley first, followed by *Homo sapiens*. How long the two groups shared the area also remains a mystery. (The best guess is fifteen thousand years or so.) Solid proof is lacking. The scene took place too long ago. The figurative files are closed. Oh, we can speculate about how they lived. We can give them names. We can describe their diet, measure soot depth in the ceiling, pick through animal bones piled on the ground. We can try and envision what the long-ago landscape looked like. But we will never unmask their thoughts. We will never understand their motivations.

Naming our creative ancestors does not unlock their primitive minds. Recognizing they had tamed fire does nothing to illuminate their fears. Understanding what they ingested moves us no nearer to their dreams. Did they dream? Did they aspire? Did they fear? Did they—these early modern humans—think as we do? Again, we will never know.

And even if one day, by some miracle, we do uncover evidence leading us to a better, more complete, picture of our forebears, we would certainly be no closer to the talented individuals who painted the pictures. It would not unlock the mind of the primeval parietal artist.

Were these painters seen as special? Did they differ from others in the clan? Or was everyone part of the process? Was everyone an artist? Were the painters men or women? (A case may be made for each, or for both.) Were these pioneering creators considered craftsmen or were they looked upon as prophets? Were they primitive priests? Or were they the prehistoric equivalents of bored homebodies?

And what was their rationale? Why did they ornament these French grottos? Again, we are obliged to speculate. Contemporary consensus maintains that the paintings were incantatory in nature, presumably attached to the hunt. According to this explanation the artwork was magically meant to guarantee a successful hunt or perhaps to provide protection for the hunters. This well may be true, but it does not explain all the images at Lascaux—the bizarre, enigmatic non-representational signs found in the Apse being the principal exception. Nor are the cave paintings merely mimetic. There are no depictions of the wild Paleolithic habitat or the ubiquitous reindeer we suspect they hunted. The images were not meant as snapshots. They were not done to mirror nature. The groupings of animals on the walls were done with a purpose in mind. There is a point to the paintings; they exist for a reason. There is rational creative thought behind them. They were done with a goal in mind. Art, from its beginning, was teleological.

Was the artwork revered in its time? Was it popular? Are the drawings evidence of totemic tribalism? Do the paintings signify the beginnings of a caste system? Are the images the dawning of narrative? Did they draw to tell stories through pictures? Perhaps—one is tempted to theorize— primeval cave art marked the first tentative step in codifying and recording cultural myths. Could the art of Lascaux be the illustrated emergence of consciousness?

There will always be too many questions. We will never know why they made these provocative drawings. Some mysteries are buried too deep.

What we do know is that the cave art of our ancestors has survived for us to question and debate and enjoy. And, though we know little, we can conclude with confidence that they created their art for a reason, even if the reason(s) forever elude us. For the making of art is not killing reindeer. Art is not catching fish. It is not gathering water nor sheltering from the cold. Art is conceptual. It is notional. Even if the artwork was done for shamanistic purposes tied to survival, it is motivation and ideation of a higher order; it is the optical concretization of abstraction.

And abstract thinking sets *Homo sapiens* on the bumpy road to civilization. For once human beings linked notional thought—and drawings, whatever the motive, are merely physical representations of notional thought—to survival or to desire, superstitiously or not, there was no turning back. Thought and action once bound will not be sundered.

Abstraction is tied to individuality. Creativity is personal. If representative thought—irrespective of physical size or speed or strength—can influence actions and events, improved thinking can lead to better outcomes. Individuals who were seen as more successful at such thinking—such divining—would be prized, deified even. They would be singled-out. They would be flattered. They would be followed. Leaders would emerge. Hierarchies would develop.

As the world does not exist until we are born into it, anonymity does not appear until individuation. Prior to individuation the idea of anonymity could not exist; there was no need; it made no sense. Survival, sex, food, life, everything was a group activity. What was good for one was good for all. There was no practical demarcation between individuals. Existence was far too tenuous. The pack lived and died as one. Only a detached, self-conscious, self-reflective *person* can distinguish I from them.

But once human beings begin to think of themselves as individuals with a figurative capital I— and more specifically, to think of themselves as unique and special—the conceptual door to anonymity creaks open. Only a somebody can aspire to be a nobody.

Given the extent and duration of prehistoric cave art there is probable cause to believe early artists were held in high esteem, that they were valued for their talents and perceived mystical powers. Additionally, and perhaps more significantly, it is reasonable to presume the admired artists over time came to accept, if not believe in, their exalted status. If present-day man is any indication, artists seldom lack conviction. They are rarely diffident about their creative gifts.

Did these early parietal artists consider creative immortality? Did they even possess the concept? Did they contemplate signing their work with an illustrative flourish or a representative symbol or a name? Did they even have names? An alphabet would not emerge for thousands of years. Were they aware they were leaving a lasting record of their existence? And, if so, would they have wanted to remain anonymous? Or was the idea of anonymity too new, too advanced, for their inchoate intellect?

In the sixth-century B.C. a Grecian by the name of Sophilos became the first human artist to take credit for his artwork by signing a small painted pot. *Sophilos drew me*, the inscription reads. A few hundred years later, Classical Greeks would originate the first theory of art built on the predictable idea of mimesis. The mysterious, dramatic and colorful walls at Lascaux were painted fifteen millennia before human beings first started to rationalize artistic creativity.

The cave at Lascaux, then, is the shared womb of

creation, its artwork the umbilical blood of many births, many human firsts. There is the birth of superstition and the birth of ego. There is the birth of creativity and the birth of storytelling. There is the birth of individualism and the birth of art.

Anonymity, too, was born at Lascaux. It was a virgin birth, an immaculate anonymity, one with no clear motivations. And maybe that is as it should be. Maybe anonymity should be, at its outset, innocently accidental. A pristine anonymity exists in Lascaux, if only because we will never know the reasons behind the creations. We are too far removed, too developed. We have become alienated from our own beginnings.

Does our admitted ignorance introduce the idea of anonymity prematurely? Are we just projecting a false innocence, a romantic naïveté on to colorful cavern walls? Do we long for a simpler time, a less noisy, less ego-centric consciousness? Perhaps. We will never know if the anonymity at Lascaux was intentional. But that does not stop us from asking questions. It does not stop us from wondering. If the anonymity *was* intentional, what does that mean? What can we learn from it? And what would this say about modern man? Would it provide a lesson in humility? Would it serve as a temporal warning? Or, sadly, have we become too self-absorbed and sophisticated to recognize the inherent beauty in unadulterated anonymity? More questions without answers.

In heuristic and historical terms, before the

cryptic cave records of the Vézère Valley, all human beings were equally anonymous. Today, early *Homo sapiens*, our distant forefathers, are lumped into a faceless, hardscrabble collection of the dirty and hirsute, a squalid unenlightened band of grunting mouth-breathers. Their lives are usually depicted as brief, severe and, apart from the admittedly important task of disseminating DNA, inconsequential. No one was special. No one remained after their heart stopped pumping. No one was remembered. No one was memorialized. Art changes this. Art reshapes our conceptions of history and humanity. The enduring power of these primitive paintings recalibrates not only our imaginative notions; it also enhances our ability to empathize with our ancestors. We recognize ourselves in this parietal art. We identify with this primal urge to create. We appreciate the appeal of the image. On some level it helps us better understand our primitive progenitors.

Generation after generation altered and added to the sacred gallery at Lascaux. The drawings were made to last. They were made for others. In some ways they were made for us. The bygone nameless artists— whether or not they wanted it—are now immortal. Their thoughts and ideas live on in us.

The cave at Lascaux was closed to the public in 1963. Too many admiring, anonymous breaths were damaging the fragile subterranean artwork.

But you can still visit the barred entrance high

above the milky Vézère. You can try to envision the scene twenty millennia before your birth. You can make the experience personal. You can make it meaningful. The soft wind whispers through the willows. A dog barks. A hunched figure—carrying a tiny flame on a flat stone in one hand and a clutch of sticks and bones and primitive pigments in the other—approaches the cave's mouth. You watch the solitary silhouette enter and move through large shadows thrown by the small fire. You follow the plodding figure through the winding passageways. After a time the shape stops in front of a white calcite wall. The open lamp and rudimentary materials are carefully placed on the ground. The cloaked figure gazes up at the blank wall and pauses. You wonder what this prehistoric mind is thinking. What goes through any artist's mind? And you imagine that it is you. Alone, wrapped in rotting reindeer hide, burning animal fat for light and heat in the cool shadows beneath the wet earth, you pick up a thin bone and touch it to the wall. The artist is you and is not you. The artist is anyone. The artist is anonymous.

DENIAL

When one door closes, you tell yourself. A stab at humor. It closes after you. The door. Not your humor. Slam.

Junk mail lies scattered, soliciting. Credit card offers and bills. How long before they know?

Termination has four syllables.

How long before everyone knows?

Your tiny studio apartment—your only meaningful possession—opens before your watery eyes; it is a premature view. Dim midmorning sunlight—strange, lazy, irregular, Wednesday midmorning sunlight—settles on your stuff: the tan sofa bed, the rectangular two-tiered coffee table, the square Formica table with matching steel chairs (2), the stunted half empty bookcase, the tall white trumpet lamp, the ancient TV on its shelved black stand, the faded fake oriental rug, the crooked Beardsley reproductions, the thin cracks climbing the off white walls, the water stains on the ceiling, DO NOT PAINT printed on the yellowing smoke detector, the gaps in the floorboards, the dust and the dirt, the grit and the grime. This is yours. Whatever they do they can't take this.

They'll stop.

You dump your things on the table and plunge deep into the couch. For a time you don't move, you don't think.

When depressed, the fat red button at the top right corner of the remote turns on the television. Red for on? You wonder. Why confuse such a simple operation? Red means stop, green means go. From time immemorial. You once read it has something to do with evolution. How? You can't remember. Add another button for Christ's sake. No can do. One chubby, dual-purpose red button for on and for off. To save space? More efficient? Laziness? Money? Yes.

Efficiency is the reason given. This is not personal. There is nothing you've done or could have done. The entire department is to be closed, absorbed, repurposed, outsourced, abolished. For the record, your work was exemplary. You were an asset, a real asset. We and the company thank you for your many years of service. Good luck.

What record? Are there files?

Of course you know there are files: paper files, electronic files, secret files: foldered files, files destined to survive long after you're dead and gone. There have always been files. There have always been records.

16

What kind of world would it be without records? How would the world function? How would people progress?

But will they doctor the files? Will the entire incident be scrubbed? Will they admit their mistake? Will they record their error? Or will they ignore it altogether?

And how will they react once the incident is revealed as an error?

An unsmiling young face will meet you in the glassy lobby and escort you to a private conference room on the seventh floor where the principal actors in your farce will be gathered. You will be offered water, perhaps a soda or a donut, refreshment. The vice president of HR will begin by extending his hand and his deepest apologies for the unfortunate—that's the word he'll use—*unfortunate* mix up. You will wince at the word. As he speaks of reconciliation he will direct several severe scowls—shooting daggers with his eyes, it is called—at his underlings, the supposed responsible parties, the buffoons who terminated the wrong person. The accused will hang their guilty heads in personal and professional shame. The HR VP will apologize for a second time in a long-winded, self-serving way and conclude by offering you an olive branch or two, maybe extra paid time off or a one-time salary bonus or both. He will claim to be very sorry for this—again he will lean on the word unfortunate— *unfortunate* series of events at which point, out of words and tired of grinning, he will turn to your vice president—the vice president of marketing services, your friend and colleague, your coworker for the past twenty-two years—and indicate that it is now her turn to speak.

Your VP, your friend and mentor, will apologize in an indirect way, emphasizing that she had nothing whatsoever to do with this business and was unaware of the error until it was too late and that it was she, as a matter of recorded fact, who first reported the mistake to Human Resources and that she never would have accepted your termination without a knockdown, drag-out war. She will make it clear to everyone in the room that should they ever even consider removing you from this company against your will they might as well let her go too. We are a team, she will say, a package, a family. And when someone in my family is injured, she will continue, it injures me. At this point she will glare long and hard at the HR VP and his cowering lackeys before warning them all that this is a troubling episode she trusts will never be repeated. The HR VP will nod in tacit agreement answering that procedures have been put in place to prevent this from ever happening to anyone ever again. He will apologize once more to you and to your VP and to all inconvenienced by this *unfortunate* happenstance.

The two HR underlings, the ones who did the deed, the ones who fired you, the ones who are being blamed for the *unfortunate* error, will then be unleashed to utter rehearsed and C-level-approved apologies for their mistake. They will cite man's imperfect nature. They will appeal to your humanity. They will beg for your forgiveness. Please accept our apologies. Please return to the company. You can't know how sorry we are. Out of words they will turn to their VP to read his face, to receive their grades.

And then it will be your turn to speak. You must give them an answer. The stage is yours. They await your decision.

You are not much of an orator but in this *unfortunate* situation you are required to say something. Yes, at the very least. You take a breath and look around the table and begin talking. The words, you realize, do not matter. What matters is your demeanor and your consent. You fight not to speechify. You read the hope, the boredom and the relief on the faces around the table. For various reasons they need you to return to the company and be happy about doing so. They want you to return. You keep talking knowing that in the end you will please them by accepting their apologies with grace and returning to the fold, like a good little lamb, back to your work, back to your department, back to your VP, back to your family.

At the end of the meeting they will express their

regrets in less formal fashion and your old identification badge and corporate smart phone will be returned. No hard feelings. You will be told to take the remainder of the day off—paid, of course—as a token of the company's collective gratitude. They will all praise the way you've handled the *unfortunate* situation. One of them will use the word aplomb. You are not sure you know the word. Hands will be shaken, backs patted. You will thank them all and explain to them that if it's all the same you'd like to get back to your desk right away. There is work to be done. For a moment they will be held in wordless awe before applauding in delight and admiration as you stride toward the shiny metal elevators.

A diseased pigeon bumps against the window and startles you. It eyes you bobbing its tiny-brained head. You watch the wind ruffle its tattered blue-gray-green feathers. You think about what it would be like to fly. It coos. You see that it's missing a toe, no, two toes. Its beak is black and brown and covered in gunk. Suddenly the bird shits white on your sill. A tap on the pane scares it away.

You check and recheck your phone for messages. You wait. You wait for them to reveal their error. You wait for them to call you back to the office. Refresh. Refreshing. Refreshed.

Attention! If you or a loved one suffers from mesothelioma as the result of exposure to asbestos contact the attorneys at Ross & Kübler immediately. You may be entitled to a substantial monetary settlement.

When the surprise—and we do realize this is a surprise, a bolt from the blue, so to speak—when the surprise of this unanticipated news diminishes—and in time it will—we feel that you will agree that this difficult decision—in the long run—is the best for all parties concerned. To this end, we are confident you will also agree that the benefit and transition package is far more than generous. Lavish one might say. The compensation and support services at your disposal have been designed to ensure your continued professional success—whatever or wherever that may be. Think of this event, then, as an opportunity for you. Opportunities, in fact. The whole world awaits. Explore. Challenge yourself. You now have the time to do those things you've always wanted to do, go where you've always wanted to go. We urge you to take full advantage of this once-in-a-lifetime opportunity. Thank you again for your service. You have our congratulations and our very best wishes.

Do what things? Go where? And do what?

Nothing on television is any good. Channel after dumb, humdrum channel. Everything is stupid. And loud. People yelling. The sickening meeting replays in your head. It's on a loop. You were too stunned to respond. You change channels. Where have all the lousy soap operas gone? And the cartoons? There's nothing. Nothing engages you. Still in shock, you figure. You press the fat red button for a second time and the screen crackles and goes gray.

You straighten a Beardsley but it sags back, crooked.

A party?! For me? You shouldn't have, you will say in all sincerity, shaking your head in mild amusement. You should not have gone to this trouble. Although early in the morning everyone will be there, even the VP. There will be an enormous, tinseled WELCOME BACK! streamer strung across the door to your office. It's like you've returned from the grave. People will be clapping and smiling. You will feel a flush of embarrassment amid the warm display of camaraderie. I don't deserve this, you will think, after all I was only gone two days. It's a little too much, isn't it, too over the top? Maybe it's important to them too.

With mock formality you will be presented an over-sized greeting card signed by your coworkers, each one having taken the time to scribble a brief note, something kind or funny or kind of funny. *How was your vacation? We missed you! Remind me, who are you again? You're back? I didn't even notice you were gone.*

You will be elbow-led into your office and on your desk will sit a flat square cake in your honor. Chocolate with creamy white icing. Flowing pink script (strawberry? raspberry?) spells out *Very Important Employee.* The cake, you will be told, is a gift from Human Resources. A sweet way to make amends, someone will joke.

White plastic forks and paper plates will appear. The VP will make a toast. Someone will cut into the cake. Another bottle of sparkling grape juice will pop. Someone will laugh.

Your best friend Chris and two others from your former department remain from the purge. They will take turns hugging you. You are comrades in arms. Chris will take you aside to talk in private. I was worried. You didn't answer. Pat, Alex and I were furious when we heard you were let go. Stunned we were. It was unbelievable. It's ironic—and lucky in a way—that this happened to you and not one of us. It was so clearly a mistake. I'm glad you're back. Next time take my calls, answer your texts. I was worried.

No, not you, it cannot be true. Not you.

Smug everyday objects stare back at you, objects you used to ignore: the blue oval centerpiece you got from your parents, an empty emerald green vase, a dusty CD rack, a ceramic owl, a plastic broom, the blinking smoke detector.

You feel ill, nauseous. You should eat something.

The phone vibrates in a small circle. You don't recognize the number. The mystery caller leaves no message.

You scrounge. Why even have a refrigerator? Who lives like this? A cheap bottle of New Zealand Sauvignon Blanc. Two warty pickles in their cloudy brine. A quart of expired milk listing in the door rack. Something smelly of indeterminate age wrapped in wax paper. Cheese? A few drops of Tabasco. A quarter-slab of rock hard butter pimpled in crustcrumbs stuck to a tea saucer. No bread. You can't make a simple slice of toast. And the cupboard? Some coffee beans. Half a sleeve of fig rolls. Sugar. Salt and pepper. A quarter jar of imperishable honey. An empty cereal bar box. You should eat something. Can't go out though. Order in? You can't go out. You might miss the call.

You shuffle over to the closest steel chair and stare at the fat folder on the table. The folder is embossed with the company logo, a glinting royal seal. You run your fingers over the ridges. You lift the folder open slowly, careful not to dislodge the contents.

Glossy pamphlets with perky, young, culturally diverse professionals greet you from deep pockets. *Expanding Your Horizons. Seizing the Day Your Way.* Behind and above the photogenic perfection stand stacks of thick bond paper rationalizing the need for efficiency, extolling the advantages of change, promoting the power of opportunity, blah, blah, blah. You see your full name in bold print.

The packet feels expensive, luxurious: the explanations, the ink, page after thick page. The paper is watermarked. And, of course, it too is embossed. Again your fingers find diversion in the raised ridges as you flip through the sheets. The linen-like crispness even sounds expensive. Cost is relative. Efficiency is relative. How many folders? How many others? You have our congratulations?

One of the pages directs you to a website.

Your laptop warms and you go to the site.

Click on the link below to access benefit package details and instructions. The link is blue and cold.

You read the instructions. You note, without much satisfaction, how HR has turned *benefit* and *severance* into synonyms. Identifying this trickery does not make you feel any better.

The blue link gives you pause. You hesitate.

Business Staffing Solutions, a national leader in contract employment, is always on the lookout for smart, hard-working, experienced professionals who value the freedom of well-paid, short- to medium-term opportunities. Click here to visit our website!

They know. That was fast.

The cold blue link gives you pause. You are afraid.

At work—yesterday, when you used to work, when you had a job—you'd never have given a second thought to clicking on the blue link. It would not have slowed you. You wouldn't have paused to consider the consequences. You would have clicked without a worry. At work, web searching was an adventure. Instant gratification. Curiosity sated. There was no fear. There was no risk. Because, you knew, behind you, backing you, somewhere in the multi-storied office block of your multi-national company lived the Information Technology department. And whatever happened, whatever ensued, whatever chaos was spawned by clicking on a queer blue link at work could always be remedied by the IT team. You were protected. Safe.

But that was yesterday. Now you are at home, alone. And it is the middle of the day. It is the middle of the work week. And you are afraid.

Click on the link below to access benefit package details and instructions.

Bugs, worms, viruses, malware, spyware, ransomware. This is what waits for you.

Ah, that's it. Of course. They took your work phone. It'll take time to find your records—your personnel file—and reach you at home, to call your personal cell. There are procedures to be followed. That must be it. You must be patient. They'll call. You cross your legs and half-smile imagining the panicked looks as HR scrambles to undo their tremendous blunder. Imagine them—your company, your colleagues, your friends—imagine them letting you go, disposing of you. Absurdity of absurdities. Imagine. You'll all have such a laugh over it. You won't blame anyone. You'll laugh. You'll laugh later. But first you must be patient.

Gold bought! Best prices! Antique, contemporary, pristine or damaged jewelry, we accept anything gold. We pay in cash! Click here for details!

They'll call soon. And they'll tell you everything

was a grave mistake. It was all in error. A clerical misunderstanding. Don't be silly. You'd never be let go.

You stare at the screen, watching the ads rotate, one after the other, as if they were reading your scared, scattered thoughts. More mail. You realize that you're being ridiculous. You aren't really afraid of malware, you are afraid to take the fatal step. You are afraid to face the unknown. Maybe if you don't click then it didn't happen, like it's a bad dream, like it's a mistake.

With wild wet eyes you ran—you recall running, pounding the corridor carpeting—to the vice president, your friend, your protector, your superior, to confirm the mistake. No one was there. Not even her assistant. Did they know? Were they in on it? Were they hiding?

A pint glass of tepid tap water, two pickles and four fig rolls. You wonder what damage Tabasco would do to a fig roll.

Refresh. Refreshing. Refreshed. Still nothing. Lunchtime after all. Later.

Click on the link below to access benefit package details and instructions.

There is no hurry. No rush. It's too soon. You

need time to process.

You look around the apartment for something to do, something to keep hands and mind busy. But in the middle of a workday Wednesday, when you are supposed to be at work working, there is no work for you here. Nothing waits to be done. Nothing waits for you. Nothing waits but the cold blue link.

The telephone buzzes. It is Chris. You can't talk now. No way. You let it go to voicemail. Beep. I just heard. I don't know what to say to you.

Same.

Pat, Alex, and then Chris again call in quick succession. You receive texts of desperation. Chris texts and texts. You don't answer. You can't.

Man barricades against himself, you once read somewhere.

You could rearrange the books. Color? Size? Topic? They look sad and neglected. You squint to read the titles. Some are strange, almost foreign. You don't remember reading them. But you must have. Could there be an unread book tucked among the others? Is it conceivable that you've read them all?

You cannot go out. But you want to. Waiting is painful and worthless. Maybe you should go outside. Get some fresh air. But you know you shouldn't. You can't. You don't have the strength to leave.

You could at least open a window. For air. For polluted city air.

Your phone buzzes again. Another pleading text from Chris, but nothing about the mistake. Still nothing from HR. Nothing from the VP. Nothing.

And let one of those filthy flying rats in?

You cannot believe it.

You find thirty-six tiny yellow tulips hidden in the swirls of your rug, a discovery after fifteen years.

You never counted before.

Afternoon becomes evening. The sunlight has moved on. Office hours are over. Your laptop sits on the table. The on button pulses white.

Unbelievable.

There is nothing more to wait for.

You cannot believe it.

You figure, then, you don't work there anymore.

You rattle the mouse and the web page reappears.

Click on the link below to access benefit package details and instructions.

You close your eyes and click.

A KING

The oldest portions of the oldest written narrative known to man, the Sumerian *Epic of Gilgamesh*, date to at least 2100 B.C. That much we know. The story is likely much, much older. It is impossible to say just how old. And its origins come to us as fragments, cracked tablets, quite literally blocks of text. Experts believe the first fragments, the earliest clay tablets, furrowed from side to side in wedge-shaped cuneiform, were in fact disparate poems celebrating the legendary king of Uruk. They were not part of a larger narrative. They were more like flash fiction in verse. These experts contend it wasn't until around 1200 B.C. that the complete cycle, the so-called Standard Akkadian version of Gilgamesh, first made its appearance.

If the story of Gilgamesh took a millennium or longer to create and arrange, it must have been recorded and rewritten by hundreds, if not thousands, of various people in various places throughout what we now call the Near East. Not one of these scribes is remembered. The names of the authors have been lost to history. They are all anonymous. The *Epic of Gilgamesh* is not signed.

But mighty King Gilgamesh—rendered as Bilgamesh in the early tablets—lives on. And that is the heart of the matter in terms of our investigation. The mere fact that we know his name, that *his* history has survived, is the story within a story. The miracle here is the saga's continued existence, its longevity, its survival. For at its core the *Epic of Gilgamesh* is about what it means to be mortal. It is a story about what it means to be human. It is a cautionary tale, one loaded with lessons.

At the beginning of the twelve tablet epic, the fearsome king of Uruk, Gilgamesh—two-thirds god and one-third man—is an abhorrent creature. He is a violent, cruel despot brutalizing and terrorizing his subjects. Among his more heinous acts is his penchant for deflowering young women prior to their marriage, his kingly right. And it is an act he relishes. He enjoys the privilege. He is beastly. He feeds off force. He revels in his power. He takes pleasure in cruelty.

This is life lesson number one: Power corrupts, absolutely.

Gilgamesh's behavior worsens. His wretched subjects increasingly plead to the gods. The pitiful entreaties eventually become too much for the gods to bear. They decide to intervene. So they create or select (the text is unclear which) the savage Enkidu, the strongest of all the wild forest men, to destroy Gilgamesh. But first the wild man must himself be tamed. This is accomplished with a six day, seven night visit from a comely temple prostitute. In ancient Mesopotamia it was sex that soothed the savage beast.

Enkidu is led to a shepherd's camp for a crash course in civilization. After a time, domesticated but not weakened, he appears at court in order to stop Gilgamesh from raping again. The two warriors fight. It is a titanic, back and forth, struggle. The duel is long and brutal. Eventually Gilgamesh gets the better of Enkidu but remarkably chooses not slay him. Gilgamesh respects the wild man's audacity and his strength. The two have bonded in battle. They become the best of friends.

This is life lesson two: Everybody, even a king, needs a friend.

The tale then follows Gilgamesh and Enkidu as they roam the kingdom fighting bad guys and getting into trouble, generally boys being boys. Seeking fame they slay the monstrous guardian of Cedar Mountain. They fell many of the magnificent trees for sport and souvenirs. They also murder the Bull of Heaven, which was unleashed by a spurned Ishtar. Gilgamesh even impudently hurls a piece of the dead bull at the angry goddess. Once again the gods are forced to intercede following this destructive, willful, disrespectful, contemptible display.

This is life lesson three: Do not anger the gods.

Death shall be the punishment, say the gods. But who's death? Should it be Gilgamesh or Enkidu? Both are complicit. After spirited debate Enkidu is chosen. Immediately the wild man becomes ill and dies an excruciatingly painful and drawn-out death while his friend, the king, watches helplessly. The mighty Gilgamesh is devastated.

This is life lesson four: Losing the one you love really, really hurts.

Grieving, Gilgamesh broods on his own mortality. Why must men die, he asks? Convinced it may be possible to circumvent the mortal death sentence, he embarks on a hunt for the secret to immortality. He travels the known world, alone, indefatigable. Eventually he reaches Urshanabi, the ferryman, who agrees to sail the king of Uruk through the waters of death. At the end of the long journey Gilgamesh alights at the edge of the world and comes face to face with Utnapishtim. (Utnapishtim is the Mesopotamian Noah, who after surviving the great flood was granted immortality. It bears mention that the tremendous rainfall, according to the tablets, was of the same duration as the prostitute's visit to Enkidu. A week must have had a power it no longer retains.) The timeless man speaks to Gilgamesh about the great deluge. He promises him that if he can stay awake for an entire week (again, that familiar time frame) he will reveal the secret to eternal life. Gilgamesh accepts the challenge but, of course, fails. And when he awakens Utnapishtim explains that all along the king's quest has been folly. There is no secret to eternal life. There is no immortality for men. The gods have willed that man must die. And that is that. He, poor, pitiable Utnapishtim is, and always will be, the only immortal, the exception, the walking talking warning.

Here is lesson five: Man must die but humankind

will endure.

On his long, sad, uneventful trek back home Gilgamesh reconciles himself to his own mortality. He remembers Enkidu. He is returning a better king, a better person. And as he approaches Uruk he pauses on a tall bluff to gaze over his magnificent city. It is there, studying the impressive, towering city walls, that he realizes therein lies the nearest he'll ever get to immortality. Human immortality is in what we build: it is in what we create, it is in what we leave behind. Immortality is what we do with our life.

And this is lesson six, the final lesson: Creating is the nearest man can get to immortality.

The anonymous *Epic of Gilgamesh* is the tale of a powerful king facing the absolute power of the gods and mortality. Gilgamesh is destined to fail. Despite being two-thirds god he will die, just like every human being who reads or hears his story.

There is recent physical evidence to suggest that Gilgamesh the king was, indeed, an actual person, a real-life historical king. Archaeologists have uncovered references to his kingdom and his fame. He may be more than legend. He may have walked the flat earth between the banks of the Tigris and Euphrates. But whether he existed in the flesh is not our primary concern. No, we are interested in the lessons of his ancient story. We are concerned with the content of the saga, not the facticity of its characters.

It is, it must be said, noteworthy that this first

recorded narrative centers on a flesh and blood human being—however partial. The main character, the protagonist, is not anonymous, anything but. He is front and center. He is on display. He is the hero. It is *his* story. Gilgamesh is not anonymous and that is the point. For fear of anonymity is our hero's ultimate weakness. Gilgamesh, the almighty warrior king, is not afraid to die; he is afraid he will be forgotten. This is what the twelve tablet saga is about at its core. This is at its heart. How does one avoid being forgotten? And, according to the epic, the simplest way to guarantee that one is not forgotten is to live forever. Physical presence ensures immortality. Would anyone dare forget the great Gilgamesh while he reigns? The solution is logically sound. Alas, immortality is impossible. And if a powerful god king is mortal, so are we all. Gilgamesh learns the hard lesson of mortality: ashes to ashes, dust to dust, nothingness to nothingness, anonymity to anonymity. Such is the unavoidable fate of all humans.

The story of Gilgamesh, then, can be read as one in a series of attempts to escape the oblivion we all face as mortal beings. And, to be sure, a powerful king has resources and powers we can only dream of. It is unsurprising that he should marshal these in a bid to remain relevant. First, he erects walls and turrets and great cities. He sires offspring. He wins battles and defeats monsters and conquers territory. He extends his fame and his name. His legend spreads. And later, in a stroke of fortuitous genius, he instructs his royal scribes to record his glory, to chronicle his exploits. The anonymous authors, his loyal subjects, forever archive his fame in poetic songs on large clay tablets.

The parapets and buildings of Uruk turned to sand long ago. Gilgamesh, if he lived at all, has been dead for at least five thousand years. Nothing remains but bird-like scratches on clay. And therein—thereon—rests his true immortality. Gilgamesh's triumph over time is that his story is still read.

Reviewed this way the *Epic of Gilgamesh* manifests a certain level of intellectual sophistication. It isn't just legend or popular recitative poetry. The saga is a symbol—many symbols in fact—of people straining to comprehend the pressures of increasing civilization. Gilgamesh represents the bad and the good, the hope and the despair, the entire psychological spectrum of newly civilized man.

If Lascaux was painted at the dawning of human consciousness, the *Epic of Gilgamesh* was written at breakfast time. The pocked tablets reflect a culture that had already mastered language and politics. Society and cities had been founded. The question the *Epic of Gilgamesh* asks is: what now? Now that human beings have food and housing and religion and commerce and society, now that we have created an advanced civilization, how do we act? How do we live? What matters? Why must we die? Why must we hurt? Humans, for the first time in history, are in a position to ask the big questions.

And through the character of Gilgamesh, the most powerful—indeed part god—man in the world, people, ordinary people, anonymous living and breathing people, could analyze and debate the questions and lessons of life. Philosophy burgeons.

Every new generation believes it is the pinnacle of intellectual evolution. We like to think we are the latest and greatest in a long line of inevitable progress. And to achieve this progress, to continue to evolve, we must shed the silly naïveté of those who came before us. As human beings we strip away the superstitions of our forefathers slowly, layer by ignorant layer. But the task is never quite complete. We are never done. There are rips and tears and patches and fixes. And sometimes we regress. Sometimes we must relearn the lesson.

The anonymous authors or editors or scribes— creators is probably the best word—of the *Epic of Gilgamesh* were millennia removed from the desperate dank caves of Paleolithic Europe. The people of Mesopotamia had the time—relatively—to reflect and consider their wants and needs, partially emancipated from tattered tribal superstitions. They had developed a language to compose a poetry that could be recalled and recorded, sung and exalted. They had a yearning to learn, a desire to understand and the freedom to do so. They asked questions. They wondered. And today we are still wondering, still asking ourselves many of the same questions. Why are we mortal? How do we get along with one another? What makes life meaningful? Even today the Gilgamesh lesson plan can help us. His story can still teach us. Not everything should be stripped away.

We remember Gilgamesh because his story is immortalized in stone. It has endured, both physically and in our collective consciousness. Gilgamesh, the god king, and Enkidu, the wild man, perished as we all must, but Gilgamesh the epic will live on long after we are gone. In a way, its anonymous authors and scribes also live on. Their work—the ancient black slabs of Akkadian phonograms—is the closest thing to human immortality we have. Together, king and storyteller erected a solid narrative edifice, a composition that has lasted. The legendary adventures and philosophies etched into the tablets are their legacy. Their lessons are timeless. And their contemporary presence is a testament to the value of their content.

Lesson learned.

ANGER

Christ! Why does it have to be so goddamned complicated? Why do they make it so hard? Assistance should at the very least assist. It's built into the stupid word. Assistance should help, shouldn't it? They should help. No, it's all repetition and blind alleys. Spinning wheels. No help whatsoever. You're not getting anywhere. They are not helping.

You want to help? Schedule an interview. Make a phone call. Open a door. You'll do the rest.

The three must-have personality traits every employer looks for!

They all know.

Why can't the goddamned Beardsleys ever hang straight!

Your parents have heard the bad news and leave long messages on your answering machine. Every day there is a new message. They are worried.

Again? It's almost the exact same form. Fill it in again? You already have that. I just typed it in. Again!

It hurts. Every single time it hurts.

41

Create the perfect resumé. Get noticed. Get hired!

All the stupid instructions. All the resources. All the *help*. It's all too much. Who works like this? It's the opposite of help. Hindrance? Is that even a word? Doesn't sound like it should be. But. Yes.

This is what happens when parents live too long. You aren't allowed to be an adult; you aren't allowed to be your own person, to stand on your own.

Why me?

You were eight years of age when the bearded doctor knocked you out with orange-flavored invisible gas. He told you what to do. You breathed and counted. You slept. You woke to see your mom beside you. Your dad was at work. Your mom had been in the chair the entire night while you slept off the gas and the operation. The bearded doctor had removed your adenoids and inserted tiny plastic tubes in your ears. While you slept dreaming of endless orange groves, he reached into you took something natural and left something artificial. Your mom stayed with you. You were afraid but did not cry.

Many weeks after the operation you went back to see the bearded doctor. Your mom took you. Your dad had to work. The doctor said everything looked fine. One of the ear tubes had fallen out on its own. You were surprised you hadn't noticed. The other would have to come out. Now. Here. In the office. You got scared. Your mom told you not to worry. The doctor told you to relax. This won't hurt, he said. Then he plunged a sharp, shiny tool into your ear canal and yanked. You were blinded. You couldn't breathe. You couldn't scream. The sudden pain had stolen your sight, your breath and your voice. You were too shocked for tears. Your mom wept for you. You were frozen. Then, little by little, the shock faded, you blinked, and your whole head throbbed. The bearded doctor proudly displayed the crusty little tube. Your breathing came back with a gasp. You cried. The bearded doctor snorted. He'd hurt you.

On the way home you told your mom that it had really hurt. I know, she said, I could tell. The doctor said that it wouldn't hurt, you said. I know, she said. Why would the doctor say that? Your mom shrugged her shoulders and said she wasn't sure but maybe it was so that you would feel less afraid. Sometimes the fear of something is worse than the something itself. He was trying to help, she said. He should not have lied, you said. No, said your mom, I don't think he should have lied.

You said nothing the rest of the way. You were still in pain. You were still hurting. You wanted to tell your dad what had happened, how much it had hurt, how the bearded doctor had lied. But when you got home your dad was not there. Your dad was at work.

You never did tell him about what had happened. And he never asked.

You were only eight when you learned that people you trust will lie to you. The operation—the insertion of the tiny plastic tubes—was supposed to make it easier to hear what people were saying. You could hear them better, but you no longer wanted to listen. You no longer trusted their words.

How can it be that you are unable to remember that sadistic doctor's name? Why can't you remember that fact? Try. Try. But you cannot. You only remember certain images: your mom, the beard, the pain, the lie.

For years, for decades, you have tried to forget about that day. After all you were only a child. It was one afternoon among thousands. And there were far worse moments, worse days. You've tried, God knows, to bury the memory next to the name. Try. But it remains. It reminds. It is a part of you.

You will never trust a man with a beard.

Network your way to your dream job. Connect. Win.

They know.

A short list of a few of your new friends—the help—some of their names:

44

Corporate Psych Services,

American Career Academy,

Mature Professionals,

Resources for Humans,

Perspectives,

The Work Works,

Online Occupational Counseling,

Us, Unemployed, Underemployed and Under Pressure (UUUUP),

LifeChange Trauma Assistance.

There are many more. They are all the same.

What's their angle anyway? They aren't social workers. They aren't volunteers. What do they get out of this? What are they making off you? Does the company pay them?

Nothing online is user friendly.

Why not Chris? Why not Alex? Why you? It should have been one of them. It should not have been you.

Your lower back aches. A brand new pain. You shift your position. You sit up and stretch. You try to pin your elbows behind your back. Get up and walk around. Stretch. Try.

They could have handled it better.

Reveal your true character. Unlock your future.

I am the user!

What type of person are you? A pissed off type, that's what type.

And there they are, you imagine, at work, working. Going out for coffee. Taking meetings. Brainstorming. Laughing, talking, living, like nothing happened, like nothing changed.

Broaden your skillset and launch an exciting new career!

Except you are no longer there. With them.

Chris claims to be working to get you back. There might be hope. There might be an opening, a way back in. You are, as they say in novels, dubious.

Every day it's the same old thing. The same login. The same websites. The same messages. The same information. The same nothing. Inertia. Is that the right word? Can inertia work in both ways? You can't remember.

Write an essay describing yourself. Illustrate both your strengths and your weaknesses. Be specific. Be creative. And, most important, be honest.

The summer between the seventh and eighth grades your parents sent you away to a Christian play camp for a week. You didn't want to go. They didn't say it but they thought you spent too much time by yourself. You needed to be out among children your own age, they didn't say. It was a hellish week. Honest.

The first night, half asleep, groggy, you stepped off the top bunk and landed with a thump on the concrete floor. You were lucky you didn't break a bone. Or unlucky? There were leeches in the lake and mosquitoes in the air. The other kids all knew one another and knew how to play capture the flag and four square. You didn't know them or the games or the rules. No one explained anything to you. You were just supposed to know. The cabin was small and dirty, crowded and loud, and the other kids were mean. One almost pushed you into the lake. Another threatened to punch you in the throat.

In the middle of the week you were made to write a letter home. You were ordered to describe all the fun you were having at camp. You were told to be specific. Honest. You wrote your parents telling them everything that had happened, was happening, in great, colorful detail. You told them about the fall, the bullies, the isolation, the leeches in the lake, and above all, the constant cruelty. In long impassioned sentences you described the daily horrors of the camp. You told them everything. You even wrote about seeing one of the counselors beat a camper in front of the entire cabin. You wrote that you wanted to come home. You asked your mom and dad to come and get you.

They didn't come. No one answered your letter. Three days later when the long week was up your parents met you in the lodge for the closing ceremony as if nothing was wrong. You entered the giant room with your little packed suitcase and coiled sleeping bag. They smiled at you. The owner of the camp thanked everyone for coming and hoped to see everyone next summer. Then they made sure every child left with something, a reminder, a token, an award. Cabin number two had won the capture the flag tournament. Cabin five had won the canoe relay. Your cabin had earned an award for best clean-up after a meal. Every child's name was called. One by one, every single child was handed an embossed certificate with a red ribbon. Some were called more than once— the camp all-stars. But they never called you. No one spoke your name. You were supposed to get a certificate, an award. You helped cleanup. But you didn't care. You felt hurt but you'd been hurting all week. Your parents asked why you didn't get called. You just shrugged your shoulders. Your dad turned red as a ribbon and told you to stand up for yourself. Your mom put an arm on your shoulder and said it was up to you. It was your decision. You left the Christian camp without a certificate, without your award. Everyone else was happy. You were happy to be leaving. It's just a stupid reminder, you told yourself. Honest.

In the car, after a long silence, you asked your parents if they'd received your letter. Yes, they had. They thanked you for writing. Dad said it was well written. Mom said it was very, um, expressive. That's the word she used, *expressive*. They said that at first, like any good parent, they were concerned, but they had contacted some of the other parents and called the camp and learned that often, especially the first time away from home, campers exaggerate in the letters home. Kids make up stuff. It's perfectly normal, said your dad.

You'd written what you'd seen, described what you'd felt. You had written the truth. Honest. And your mom and dad hadn't believed you. They'd believed the others. You asked for help. And they chose not to help you.

Imagine you are a corporate brand. What makes you special? Who are your customers? Why do they need you? Now get out there and market yourself!

They are all in this together. They are all against you. Just in different ways, on different levels.

The news taunts you. A special report confirms that the economy is picking up. Unemployment is down. The nation has turned a corner. The worst is over. You want to laugh.

The seven (ssh!) secrets to success.

Entertainment mocks you. You watch filthy rich people complain about nothing. A baseball star signs a hundred million dollar contract. Sitcom actors hold out for a million per episode. Five hundred thousand per just isn't enough.

Music laughs at you. You stop on MTV but you don't recognize anything. There's no singing. They all use their hands too much. And they're all angry at something or other. Why even wear pants? Teenaged punks playing with money and drugs and guns. Why are they all so angry? Gangstas, they call themselves.

They do not understand.

And bitches.

Act now, they warn. Like you'll miss the only opportunity you'll ever have. You'll answer when you're good and ready.

Your presence bothers you. Your body. You

don't like what you're becoming. You're angry too.

Make yourself indispensable in nine easy steps.

You become louder. You need to be heard. You yell at the television. You scream into the telephone. You holler out the window. It's okay to be angry, isn't it?

This is such a waste of time. This cannot be right.

You've done what they asked. You have virtual assistance. You've made virtual contacts. The assistants call themselves counselors or employment consultants and have phony names like Flo Enright and Pierce Webb. It is hard to believe the names are real, hard to believe they are real, hard to believe there's an actual person somewhere on the other side of your computer screen, at the other end of miles and miles of wire.

No one really understands. They couldn't possibly.

They all have the same chipper demeanor and the same recommendations, the same hollow results.

You deserve a little respect, after all. You've earned that much.

It's not help. They're all ads. It's all a con. They're taking, not giving. They want your business. You are revenue.

Why me?

Is it too much to have them respect your pain? Couldn't they at least acknowledge your suffering?

The five questions every job seeker should ask in an interview.

You can't even get an interview. You can't get a foot in the door. The doors are closed, locked tight.

The whole process is making you less of a human being. It is isolating, dehumanizing. There is nothing natural about it, nothing normal. It is clicks and forms and sharing and waiting. And nothing.

You can hear them laughing.

No one is listening.

Are they going to hurt or help?

You are not going to change who you are to suit them. You are not going to change your language. They can't take that away from you.

They can go to hell! That is what they can do. They can go straight to hell! Every goddamned one of them!

A MESSIAH

It is generally recognized among scholars that the four gospels of the New Testament, the canonical gospels—literally, *good news* in Greek—were, despite titular attributions to the contrary, the work of late first- or early second-century anonymous authors. Despite the beliefs and prayers of the faithful, the texts are not the eyewitness accounts of Jesus' life written by apostles or those close to them. They are later productions. In fact, the existence of the four books is not even mentioned until the mid-second century.

The earliest of the gospels, Mark, could not have been composed prior to sixty-six or seventy A.D. (The author references Nero's persecution of the Christians in Rome and the Jewish revolt, events occurring in the latter half of the first century.) Anyone old enough to have walked with Jesus would not have lived long enough to learn of these later events. This is but one proof. There are many such anachronisms and textual problems in the canonical gospels, enough to fill a library, including, perhaps the most revealing clue of all, the fact that all four gospels were written in the third person. Surely a beholder to the seminal events in the life of the Savior Jesus Christ would have, at some point, written it down in the first person. No, these accounts were composed, not recalled. They are at least a generation or two removed from the described incidents, the life and death of Christ.

In historical point of fact it wasn't until 185 A.D. when Ireneaus of Lyons argued for the promotion of the four gospels that they were considered at all, let alone considered special. Ireneaus was the one who claimed the four texts contained the literal truth. He was convinced of their importance. And he staked his reputation on it, cleverly and eloquently, comparing them to the four winds and the four corners of the earth. Due to his passionate support and immense influence, the gospels were deemed the four pillars of the Christian Church. And it is then, and only then, that Matthew, Mark, Luke and John become the canonical cornerstones of Christianity, the building blocks of the new religion. The authorial attributions, whenever they were added, were most likely inserted to confer an apostolic imprimatur on the adopted texts. It was an easy way to separate approved inspired writings from the scores of apocryphal Christian texts circulating at the time.

Despite the so-called synoptic problem—significant textual variations and conflicts in the stories, particularly among the first three gospels—each of the four books analyzes the life and death and works of Jesus Christ. But, you ask, why would the Church need *four* separate versions of the Messiah's life and teachings? Why not just one? Why not a single authoritative version? The answer is that each gospel is told from a different perspective by a different author for a different purpose and to a different audience. The common good news is that the Messiah was born and sacrificed and resurrected for *your* salvation. Jesus Christ the Redeemer died for *your* sins. The four gospels are a united call to faith, a summons to rally behind the one true church founded on the teachings of the Lord.

In the span of a single millennium our anthropological assay has gone from the mighty, mortal Gilgamesh, one-third man, two-thirds god, to Jesus Christ of Nazareth and Bethlehem, the scraggly bearded, itinerant Son of God and Son of Man, man and god in one.

The Gospel According to Matthew

The first book of the New Testament is the Gospel According to Matthew. Its anonymous author was most probably a male Jew familiar with the abstruse legal issues of the time and one who had a competent command of synagogue Greek. Composed in the late first century, the book borrows heavily from Mark. Employing a historical approach, Matthew stresses the divine nature of Jesus, a divinity present from birth (like Gilgamesh) and illustrates how the Messiah and his followers, the believing Jews, were roundly rejected by an indifferent or persecutory Israel. The gospel reflects the struggles and strife between the author's community and the non-Christian Jews. The text is an overt warning to all Jews that they must either reject or accept Jesus Christ as the Second Coming, the Messiah. There is no middle ground.

Matthew wants them to accept Christ. And to that end he emphasizes Jesus' place within the Jewish tradition. He seeks to persuade his fellow Jews to accept Christ. The Gospel According to Matthew is a gospel written by a Jew for other Jews, for Jewish Christians. The gospel's primary concern, then, is that the Jewish tradition not be lost in an increasingly gentile church. The friction and discord Matthew depicts is among Jews themselves. The gospel attempts to answer a purely Jewish question. So our evangelical author characterizes Jesus as a continuation, not a rupture. For the author of Matthew, Jesus Christ is the fulfillment of Old Testament prophecies and must be accepted as such by all God-fearing Jews. This is the Gospel of Matthew According to Anonymous.

The Gospel According to Mark

Whoever wrote Mark wrote very poor Greek. This criticism is universal. And, for this reason and others, most scholars readily reject the tradition that ascribes the gospel to Mark the Evangelist, a companion of Peter. Like all four gospels the author of Mark is anonymous. The text relies on a variety of sources and was most likely written between sixty-six and seventy A.D. As Matthew was written for the Jews, Mark was written for the gentiles.

This earliest gospel portrays Jesus as a heroic man of action. One, who through parables and ambiguities, keeps his identity as the Son of God hidden, even from his disciples. Mark's Jesus preaches and performs miracles in preparation for the inevitable and immanent cataclysmic events of the apocalypse.

Mark bridles history for the sake of theology. His *good news* is fundamentally a theological message. He describes Jesus' life in eschatological and apocalyptic terms, depicting the Messiah as caught up in real events at the end of time. Mark is a call to action. And the gospel was written primarily for Christian members to strengthen their faith while countering a fringe of miracle-believing Greeks. Mark portrays Jesus as the suffering, mortal Son of Man. This is the Gospel of Mark According to Anonymous.

The Gospel According to Luke

Luke is the second longest of the four gospels and was probably written between eighty and one hundred A.D. Scholars term the Gospel According to Luke a salvation history. It was meant to be read aloud and therefore assumes a fairly educated audience.

Experts are convinced that the anonymous author of Luke is also the author of the Acts of the Apostles. Together Luke-Acts make up almost twenty-eight percent of the New Testament. This author was most certainly a learned Greek male, but one who respected manual labor. The Gospel According to Luke is really a narrative rather than a gospel. Its goal is to convey that God's purpose is seen in the way He has acted and will continue to act in history.

The formative shape of Luke-Acts demonstrates the universalities of the divine plan and shifts of authority from Jerusalem to Rome. Luke-Acts is about enlarging the church. The two books share a parallel architectural structure.

In Luke, theology is expressed primarily through plot. It is an historical narrative beginning with creation and brought to the present day. It is a storyteller's gospel.

Luke also stands apart from the other gospels in its emphasis on the importance of the Holy Spirit.

In sociological terms, the author of Luke needed to define the positions of Christians in relation to the two dominant distinct political and social entities of the time: the Roman Empire and Judaism. His message is that powerful rulers of this temporal world obtain their power from Satan. Such plenty and power are illusory and will lead to spiritual ruin. The loyalty of Christ's followers is to God above all else. Furthermore, although Jesus and his early followers were Jews, the continuing Christian mission and its future, in Luke's view, now lay with the gentiles. This is the Gospel of Luke According to Anonymous.

The Gospel According to John

John the Apostle was known as the beloved disciple and the Gospel According to John mentions a beloved disciple of Jesus. And thus the attribution. Unfortunately most of the apostles were beloved and this gospel, like the other three, was written by someone else, someone who will forever remain anonymous.

John was written during the church-synagogue debate of circa one hundred A.D. and is divided into four sections: Prologue, Book of Signs, Book of Glory, and Epilogue.

The Prologue of John is where the word is made flesh. It is the gospel of logos, an admixture of coopted ideas from Judaism's Lady Wisdom and Greek philosophy. The prominence of logos and light also indicates a Gnostic influence. The Book of Signs addresses Jesus' ministry and the Book of Glory revolves around the Passion and the Resurrection.

John is more hostile to the Jews than the other three anonymous gospels—there is an overt, intentional and institutional progression at work in the ordering of the four books—and John represents what we would call high Christology. John is a markedly individualistic gospel emphasizing a person's individual relationship with Jesus Christ the Divine Savior in opposition to the corporate nature of the Church. In John, Jesus is open about his divinity and the chief theme is that Jesus is the embodiment and source of eternal life (echoes of Gilgamesh). And this is our final gospel, the Gospel of John According to Anonymous.

The four canonical gospels can be summarized thusly:

Matthew: A messianic prophecy written by a Jew to Jews for Jews with Jesus as the Son of David;

Mark: Composed for Romans and portraying

Jesus as the ideal servant (*For the Son of man also came not to be served but to serve, and to give his life as a ransom for many.* 10:45) of God.

Luke: Penned to promote the humanity of Jesus as the Son of Man and to reinforce that to be Christian is to be gentile.

John: Written to prove the deity of Jesus and the eternal glory in faith (*Now Jesus did many other signs in the presence of the disciples, which are not written in this book; but these are written that you may believe that Jesus is the Christ, the Son of God, and that believing you may have life in his name.* 20:30-31).

The selection and ordering of the four gospels in the New Testament by Ireneaus and other early Christian church leaders suggests that the original despairing death of Jesus has become more and more victorious over time. It is a triumph of theology over history. Regrettably the story of Jesus also becomes more hostile to the Jewish people.

Why, in the end, would such significant works be unsigned by their real authors? And why such clumsy attributions? There are four possible reasons. The first is that the message is more important than the messenger. Anonymous authorship can be seen as an act of literary prostration at the ivory feet of the divine. But then why attribute them to someone else? This is the second reason. An apostolic attribution confers immediate authority. There were hundreds of texts in circulation in the early days of Christianity. A fragment allegedly written by an apostle, or even by someone who was the companion of an apostle, achieved instant credibility. The third possible reason for not claiming authorship is that there was no need. The writers were in a real sense working for the Lord. It was His work. A signature may have been considered blasphemous. The gospels are the sanctified stories surrounding the life and death of Jesus, not the inventive work of some penman. And the final possibility for the anonymous nature of the gospels is that they were seen as a continuation of the anonymous sacred history of the Old Testament: anonymity as religious writing tradition.

Jesus' final week occupies one-third of the four gospels. But the authors of the gospels—the textual cornerstones of the New Testament—whoever they were, were not on hand to witness that momentous week of sacrifice and salvation. They did not attend the Crucifixion. They did not observe the Resurrection. That was not their lot. They were meant to be religious writers. They were the anonymous, after-the-fact, faithful servants laying the groundwork and spreading the message of a new salvation and a new church. They were the devout anonymous vessels of God. These are the Gospels According to Anonymous.

BARGAINING

You're sitting on an empty street corner holding out your hands, your palms are up. Unemployment, disappointment and isolation have turned you into a beggar, just another nameless, faceless loser shouting from the shadows.

You don't go out. You beg indoors.

You're asking for a chance, not a limb.

Quid pro quo is the Latin. That for this? No. This for that, right? Tit for tat. The only Latin you know, the only Latin you've ever known. Who needs to know Latin?

Tat for tit: ink on a breast.

Sure, you'd learn Latin if it would help. Yes you would. You'd try anyway. Whatever it takes.

If only you'd get the chance. One chance. No need for a second.

You beg from the relative comfort of home, reclining on your sofa with the computer on your lap and a half-empty half-pint of vodka in your hand.

You have everything you need to be a beggar, including the guilt.

It is not going well.

The crooked Beardsleys are losing their contrast. The rug is stained.

It would be so easy for them. Risk free almost. And you'd do anything. You'd show them.

One chance. Anything.

You started off as a temp. You did what they asked. You rose through the ranks, as they say, for twenty years. It worked out until it didn't.

You did what they asked. You followed the directions, rewrote your resumé, drafted cover letters, researched the marketplace, asked the questions. What more do they need? What more do they want?

This should not be so difficult. It should not take so long.

The mattress tucked into your sofa stays hidden. You sleep on the lumpy seat cushions.

You participated. You are participating. You are

one of them. You are like them.

To have to begin again.

It's been weeks.

You've become so many different people, so many invented people—people is the wrong word, more like stories, characters, wishers, avatars, pseudonyms, hopefuls—that you don't know who you are anymore or who you want to be. You don't like any of them. They're all desperate whiners. Beggars.

At your age. Some would call you old. Others would consider you young.

Pat and Alex have stopped calling and texting. They've forgotten you.

You were promised opportunities. You were told you could do whatever you wanted to do.

You snubbed them. Pat and Alex.

You just want an opportunity. One stupid chance.

Out of shame.

You've been wearing the same soiled gray sweatpants and smelly orange tee shirt for three days. You stink. What if someone came to the door?

Your parents are worried.

Let's make a deal!

What if they came to check up on you?

What if an offer presented itself, like a bolt from the blue? What if an opportunity knocked on your door?

Marketing. Door to door.

Marketing. Online.

You are a brand. Market yourself!

The ads? The never-ending ads. Ad is short for advertisement. Four syllables. Short and long. Is the accent on the first syllable or somewhere in the middle? You've heard it pronounced many ways. Mispronounced. Not the end. No.

People lie.

Maybe one of the ad-ver-tise-ments is your

66

answer, an answer hidden among the many, waiting to be found. It could be fate trying to tell you something, the gods of fortune and marketing. Answer the ads. Answer the ads. Answer.

What's the use?

Ring, dammit! Ring.

You have to stick to the program, too many ads anyway, too many to select from. Do what they say. Listen to the professionals. Stay the course. You're doing great. You're doing what they want, what they ask of you. You're following their instructions to the letter. They couldn't ask for more.

Hidden comfort.

You so want to be one of their toothy success stories.

But you're getting nowhere. Playing the game should get you somewhere. You should see some progress, a tiny reason to hope. You are paying your dues, which should make them more likely to help you. If they can. If they wanted to. They. Whoever. Whomever? Whatever.

Losers.

All the counseling and the sharing and the chatting in the cyber-rooms is meant to help make you stronger, meant to make you more marketable. The conversations are supposed to help you realize that you're not alone. It is not the end of the world. But they're all the same, the chatterers and their sour words. Whatever the room, whatever the rules, everyone whines about their situation. Everyone bitches. Everyone begs.

Misery loves a chat room.

It is not fair.

Earn $5,000 or more every month! From the comfort of your home!

You know the longer you stay like this the worse it will get. You are losing ground. You are no longer in motion. You're slowly dying faster, day after dismal day. Falling. Flailing. You'll take anything. You've got to get through that first door. You promise you won't ask for anything more.

Is there a point of no return? Do you have an employment shelf life?

It was the only real job you ever had.

Stagnation: a country of male deer. Your mom would call that droll.

The studio apartment is shrinking, closing in on you. A cavern. The cracked walls chew at your sticks of furniture, the rug chomps at your floorboards, the ceiling swallows your light. It was small to start with. Now smaller.

You have no skills. Nobody wants what you're peddling.

You stop fighting the darkness. You don't turn on the lights or open the blinds. The computer screen glows, the television flashes, casting shadows.

No does not always mean no. Circumstances can change. People can change. People can change their mind.

Sometimes you hear the filthy diseased pigeons on the sill, scratching and gurgling. Dying.

You played with your neighbor's CB radio after school the year you turned twelve. You pretended you were others, you pretended you were older, pretended to warn the truckers on I80 about the smokies up ahead. You picked up their lingo. You laughed when they replied 10-4. Sometimes they got angry, said they were coming after you. You'd shut off the radio and hide in the dark. The CBers used to have such funny names. They called them handles.

Now they call them user names.

The woodcutter's axe begged for its handle from the tree. The tree gave it. What the hell is that supposed to mean?

Most of the handles spoke with fat-bellied countrified accents, chubby cheeks stuffed with tobacco. You imagined them with beards.

Some loser posted it in a chat room. It doesn't sound encouraging. It doesn't sound very supportive. Suicidal.

You are now the sad sorry owner of a half dozen user names in a half dozen cyber-rooms. You'll soon need a spreadsheet to keep them straight. But you're not laughing. No one's joking now.

Too many handles, not enough drawers. Your dad would roll his eyes.

An offer can come from anywhere.

You are past your prime.

Mail falls through the slot and spills to the floor. No hope there. No offers. Just bills. And ads. More ads. Advertisements.

More marketing.

Everyone, everything is for sale. Begging for business.

You're not even sure who (whom?) to ask. Everybody? A blanket plea. Cast a wide net they say in the chat rooms. Leave no stone unturned. But you can't waste your energies on every possible lead. You can't sell yourself everywhere. It has to be right, the right person, at the right organization, at the right time. The perfect pitch.

Desperate? Tried everything? Give us a try. Sure Staffing, Inc. guarantees placement. You have our word on it. What do you have to lose? Click here!

Click on the ad? Sure, staffing.

Now has to be the right time. It has to be now. Or soon. You are running out of time. Who do you ask? Whom?

You can't do a thing.

No doesn't have to mean no. The one constant is change or so goes the saying. Or has that changed? Like that time your mom and dad wouldn't let you go to the party at the cabin. The senior year party. No, and that's final, said your dad. You're too young. So you did the laundry and the lawn and the dishes for two whole weeks and tried again. You asked nice. You had softened them up. The answer became a yes. You'd earned the yes. People change. People change their minds. They can be made to change their mind.

The party sucked.

Ring.

The cracks on your walls are climbing, like they're trying to reach something, like they have a goal, like they're trying to escape the dark cave.

Get away from the computer. Get off the couch. Your back aches again. Your legs are sore. You should straighten the apartment. Patch the cracks. Wash the floor. Vacuum the rug. Do something.

You have no real skills. You work hard. You are a hard worker, but you have no skills.

You look in the mirror and do not like the slobby (Is that a word? It should be.) slouching (?) person looking back at you. Who would help this person, this gross thing?

Some of your current handles—your online user names—are:
Work4S,
MktngMaven12,
Star4Hire171,
CutAftr20,
Illdrnk2that2,
PgnsRDrtyRats.

Everybody is unique, an irregular goddamned snowflake.

Squatting in your dingy apartment you look homeless. A hermit.

Melting.

Do you think you are funny?

You should take a shower.

You once promised a lover that if they took you back you'd never cheat again. You pleaded and cried and promised. And you won. They took you back. Then you broke your promise. You cheated. Again.

This is different. This time it will be different.

The last time you had sex? With another person?

This is only a stage, just a phase, they say. Unemployment is one stage of your life. How long it lasts varies, they say.

All the world's a goddamned stage. That's Shakespeare. Almost. That much you know. You suspect that they know it too.

The telephone does not ring. No one texts.

You put on airs. Why? Who are you trying to fool?

Is this your true personality? Is this who (whom?) you really are?

Have you always been a fake? You've never thought about that before. Never had the time or (nor?) the reason.

Be careful what you wish for is a stupid saying.

You'd wear a hair-shirt if it would get you in the door. And you're doing it again. Showing off. You don't even know what a hair-shirt is. Something religious? Something painful? Is it a form of self-torture? Is there a way to pay for your sins?

Your resumé is out there in the ether, circulating. Is anybody reading it?

Let me file that, you used to say, before you threw it in the trash.

Are you too old to learn new tricks?

You want to call the VP and beg her for help. Is she the one? No, not her. She's against you. She's not for you. You wouldn't be in this position if not for her. She's always been against you. Plotting.

Like a dog.

You sleep on the sofa (couch?). The bed stays hidden.

Too old?

You deserve this, don't you? All of it.

Clear your mind.

Read a book. Go outdoors. Get a hobby. Do something. Didn't one of the sites tell you to develop your outside interests?

Outside. Out of doors.

Why do people climb rocks? Mountains you understand, but rocks?

Chat? In a chat room?

Race walking.

Be honest. Be honest with yourself.

Mountains are just big rocks.

The cracks climb. Up. Not down. Sometimes they go sideways.

Avoidance? Hindrance? Ance words. Who would hire you? Today. Right now.

Toward the light?

The fact that you are even considering clicking on the ad shows your level of desperation.

You are a nuisance. Another ance word.

The countless words you do not know, all these

muddled ideas and concepts, dates and names. You could look them up. You're on the computer all day long. Look them up. Educate yourself. Help yourself a little. Do something.

Isn't that still pretending?

Nobody responds to desperation. Do they? Why should they?

You stare at the phone for hours praying for it to ring. But you can't make it ring. You need help. Ring. Ring.

It's ugly. Desperation is ugly.

Miracles happen. Yes, they do. They happen every day. All the time. Why not to you? You can do something to make one more likely, can't you? You can make yourself more worthy of a miracle, can't you?

You must eat better. And you're drinking way too much. Water turned to wine turned to cold vodka. Too early. Destroys the appetite. To sleep you tell yourself. To wake. To feel or not to feel. No one wants to look at the sick. No one wants to help the sick. You're turning into a dirty animal.

You're not hopeless. You just need help, a leg up,

a chance.

Show them you are worthwhile. Show them you are deserving.

You have little choice. You have no power. You are out of options. Nothing is working. You have to do something. Someone has to help pull you out of this, help you climb out. This cannot continue.

You'll do anything. Take anything.

Help is on the web? Help is on the way?

Just a chance. You're only asking for a chance. Begging for a chance.

The world wide web? The Internet. Like the climbing lines on your walls. You are surrounded by webs. Stuck in the web. Awaiting the arachnid.

You could have used the word spider. It's simpler, easier, more you. Is arachnid even correct? Arachnophobia. Fear of.

You're tired from doing nothing. You lurch from the couch to the table back to the couch. Tired from nothing.

Networking is work. Work is right there in the middle of the word. Networking takes work. It takes time and commitment.

You should socialize. You should. But with real people. Chris keeps asking you to dinner. What can it hurt? You should go. Still trying to help. You could ask Chris? No, Chris is not the one. There'd be no point.

You promise you won't ask for a second one. Just a first. That's all you need.

You'd have to shower. You'd have to get dressed. You'd have to make small talk and chit chat. You'd have to pretend.

If you are good, you will be rewarded.

You have one remaining real friend. You push them away.

Who owes you? Are there people in your debt? Sure. But this is too big. Your old friends can't do it. And none of these online people—if they are real people—seem to have any clout. They're pathetic. They're pawns too. Cogs. Rabble. Fellow beggars.

No one should see you like this.

You don't know the definition of rabble. Admit it. Be honest.

For how long?

What's a beggar without pity?

You'd sacrifice it all for a chance.

You would even take something temporary, something short-term, something low-paying, an internship. Start from scratch, start from the very bottom. Anything.

You'd give them a kidney, if they asked.

At your age? A foot in the door. An entry-level position. The chance to prove yourself. Again.

Is there time enough to work your way back? Do you have the energy?

For weeks you've been begging the wrong people. Like a bum panhandling in a slum. No tin cup, just scaly, outstretched hands. You don't know how to ask. You don't know who (whom?) to ask. You don't know what you're doing. You've never had to beg before.

When you get an interview—when you've earned your interview—you'll tell them you are driven, driven to succeed. You'll tell them what a hard worker you are. They won't ask about your skillset. You can get the job done. Whatever that means, whatever it takes.

Your mom and dad want to help. They leave voicemails. They want to help you. Their only child.

Has anyone ever really been helped by someone in a chat room? Could you one day actually chat with somebody who can help, somebody who can offer you a job? That's a fantasy. You're pretending again.

Has *anyone* ever been hired in a chat room? Or is it a cyber space built for words, there to make you feel better, to boost your confidence? Is it only for chatting? Chat therapy.

You'd make a deal with the devil himself. On his terms. A chance is all you're asking for.

Your parents are begging too, but in a different way and for different reasons. For their only child.

Open up. Talk to more *people*. Talk to everybody. In a room. Chat. More. Make new friends. Internet friends. What do you have to lose?

Maybe you should get a pet. A dog. Or a cat. Fish? Not a bird, though. No birds.

The peregrine falcon is the world's fastest bird.

You'd keep it a secret. No one needs to know. It can be a secret deal. You won't be sorry. You'll see.

They kill pigeons, don't they?

You promise to dedicate your entire life to the new company. You promise to work tirelessly, round the clock, weekends. Vacation days? Who needs them? You'll never get sick. And you promise to die in your office chair and let them donate your body to the charity of their choice. You will live and breathe and die for them.

You just need a chance.

You deserve a chance?

Nobody deserves this.

For a chance. You're only asking for one little chance.

One interview. One door to open.

A MODEST PROPOSAL

A millennia and a half after the New Testament was assembled and approved the Christian religion and its Holy Bible were being used as pretexts for exploitation and savagery. Henry VIII in his monomaniacal break with Rome had declared war on all Catholics. Christian dehumanized Christian. The good news of Matthew, Mark, Luke and John brought little peace to the British Isles.

And by the early eighteenth century, mighty, voracious, ostensibly pious England was, in practice, systematically destroying Irish culture and the Irish people in the name of mercantilism, empire and religion. It was a particularly cruel neighborhood colonialism. The Emerald Isle and its people were divided and subjugated. In less than two hundred years despotic British Protestant hegemony had reduced much of Ireland's indigenous population to beggardom. The Irish were a defeated and demoralized people, viewed by the occupying British as little more than bothersome animals.

Some English, particularly the educated Anglo-Irish born and raised in Dublin, rejected the attitudes and policies of an uncaring London. Some worked to improve the situation of the Irish. Some tried to help the poor, to right the wrongs. Some fought. And some used language as their weapon.

Jonathon Swift (1667-1745), poet, satirist, political

pamphleteer, and essayist, is regarded as the foremost prose satirist in the English language. Even his fiercest critics call him great. His literary impact is beyond measure. His works are classics: *Gulliver's Travels, A Tale of the Tub, An Argument Against Abolishing Christianity, Drapier's Letters*, and, of course, *A Modest Proposal*. His words live on. His style is emulated around the world. His name has been turned into an adjective: Swiftian. And every single one of his many works was originally published anonymously.

Swift, for reasons both public and private, aimed his pen at powerful London, at the haughty English, and at the farcical, bombastic beliefs of his times. Though he was born in and spent most of his life in Ireland, Swift was an Englishman, a protestant, cultured and elite. He didn't much care for living in the Irish backwater. But he detested London for making his backwater worse. He thought politicians fools and reformers idiots. That said, he harbored no romantic illusions about the destitute Irish. He didn't much care for them either. He didn't believe in Irish nationalism. He didn't believe the Celts were better than their oppressors. He found the natives just as depraved. He despised all equally. His enmity was universal. His targets were those who failed to open their eyes to this truth.

Satire is best served dry and unadorned. And because the greatest prose satirist in the English language knew this better than most, Swift always published his work anonymously or pseudonymously. A Jonathon Swift-signed work would tip his hand prematurely; it would give up the game before it had begun. There were also other, more practical considerations for hiding behind the cloak of anonymity. Libel laws were broad. Politics was a blood sport. Imprisonment and worse were real, immediate dangers for an uncompromising satirist in the early eighteenth century. And Swift was the best and the most audacious. Masking his identity was imperative. If the Four Gospels—and perhaps we should include Homer here as well—represented the tentative beginnings of pseudonymity, Swift is its apogee.

A Modest Proposal for Preventing the Children of Poor People in Ireland from Being a Burthen to Their Parents or Country, and for Making them Beneficial to the Publick was written in 1729 as a Juvenalian satire. (Juvenalian satire is more contemptuous and abrasive than its cousin the milder, gentler, more light-hearted Horatian satire. Juvenalian satires attack. Horatian satires play.) The thirty-two paragraph piece is deadpan, biting, straight-faced satire with sustained irony. At its crux *AMP* wryly suggests that the impoverished Irish might ease their economic troubles by selling their children as food to the upper classes. It is presented as an elegant and straightforward solution.

The relatively short piece begins with the plight of starving beggars in Ireland's streets described in an ultra-detached manner; we witness begging women followed by *three, four or six children, all in rags*. It is a brilliant example of paralipsis. In his opening paragraph Swift implies that the author is odious and the Irish are to be pitied. It is a set-up, a feint. And one which serves at least two purposes. The first is that it allows the reader to sympathize with the downtrodden Irish and, second; the reader begins to dislike the unfeeling author of the proposal. The Irish are powerless and the author is a jerk, too dispassionate, too clinical. In one brief paragraph the reader has been hooked, rhetorically speaking.

The author of this sober proposal continues over the next few sections to describe the deplorable state of the island while presenting some benefits of his—yet unnamed—proposal. This is followed by a series of cold calculations which puts the number of newly born poor Irish at a conservative one hundred and twenty thousand per annum. And we are reminded of their lack of value.

Swift now has us ready for the grand solution, but not before alluding to the fact that the author's idea was suggested by a verbal amuse-bouche delivered by an anonymous American on the utter deliciousness of a well-fed one year-old, *whether stewed, roasted, baked, or boiled*.

Thus our author offers, humbly, that one hundred thousand Irish yearlings be offered up for sale to *persons of quality or fortune*. The remaining twenty thousand—a quarter of them male—would be reserved for breeding, which, as our author points out, is the same percentage successfully used by English cattle farmers.

Swift then sets out to sell the program. And he relies heavily on calculations. There is always more math, more unimpeachable proof. A child born at a weight of twelve pounds should, all things considered, reach twenty-eight pounds by the end of year one. A substantial dish. In turn a mother can expect to net eight shillings profit per sale. A significant sum. The Irish are described throughout *AMP* in language ordinarily reserved for farm animals.

He admits the meat will be dear, making it *proper* for landlords. The thriftier are also reminded that a child's soft skin may be used to fashion gloves or boots. One wonders what may be made of the bones.

The magnanimous author also generously mentions that many friends have helped him with his proposal and have even sought to improve upon it by suggesting that, in order to preserve good hunting, the twelve to fourteen year-old Irish be employed to replace England's dwindling deer population. Our author dismisses this proposal on the very rational grounds that older flesh is known to be *tough and lean,* but admits there is some merit in devouring teens.

Swift's hyper-logical, anonymous author highlights six important benefits to his program:

One: It will reduce the number of Papists.

Two: The poor will be paid so they can in turn pay their British landlords.

Three: It will allow money to circulate among the Irish and increase the national income.

Four: Mothers will be relieved of the burden to maintain their children after the first year.

Five: Empty taverns will be filled with customers.

Six: It will be a great incentive to marry and will increase care and tenderness of a mother to her children.

The modest author of this modest proposal admits that there are many other advantages to be found in his solution, but for the sake of brevity declines to enumerate them.

Dublin itself, says the author, would take twenty thousand carcasses. The rest may be distributed elsewhere, though children should not be raised for export. And apart from differing on distribution percentages or, admittedly, the inevitable population decrease, there can be no objection to such a reasonable and pragmatic plan. In fact our author shall entertain no other solutions nor does he want to hear talk of them unless they can address the immediate need to feed and house one hundred thousand poor. Case closed.

Swift ends the proposal by confessing that the author has no personal interest in promoting his idea, adding that he has nothing else to offer as his youngest child is already nine and his wife past the age of child-bearing. The modest author's sole contribution is his progressive, humanitarian idea.

The early eighteenth century was an age of satire, an age of argument and an age of grand plans. Swift was at the center of an increasingly industrial society and his *Modest Proposal* was aimed at many targets. It is a moral-political argument carried out by means of parody. His hyperbole unflinchingly mocks the heartless attitudes toward the poor, as well as the brutal British policy toward the Irish. It is also a general criticism of the belief—a belief pervasive at the time—that *the people are the riches of the nation*. No child was too young to work. Laborers were roundly regarded as commodities. Ergo, *AMP* was also a critique of blind mercantilism. It is a condemnation of greed. The rich in the industrial age feed off the poor, almost literally. Economically, the wealthy estate and factory owners have by this time already consumed the poor Irish children's parents. They might as well finish off the family by dining on the children. Words are Swift's weapons and he is a merciless combatant.

Many critics maintain that his principal target was not conditions in Ireland, but rather the simplistic can-do spirit of the times, a belief that led to preposterous propositions. *AMP* also targets the calculating way people perceived the poor in designing their projects, thus targeting reformers in general. Denying the Irish their natural rights and dehumanizing them had become a British pastime. But there were many well-meaning and absurd attempts to right this wrong. Too many. The idea that there was a solution, a single great answer, is another of Swift's targets. Indeed, the proposal parodies the notion of the grand idea and mocks the belief that society's ills can be solved or cured through the application of simple calculations.

The work is also a personal attack or rather—for Swift was by nature misanthropic—a number of attacks. He lampoons William Petty and his social engineering. It is a riposte to *The Generous Projector* (1728) written by Defoe, Swift's chief rival. And there are others too. *AMP* is aimed at the particular as well as the general.

Anonymous wrote *AMP*. And being anonymous the author could afford to be as scathing as he wanted. The references to others and the attack on the crown would not have gone unnoticed; they would not have missed their intended targets. Any return of fire, however, was destined to fail, for there is no one to attack. There is no one there. The only target is invisible anonymity.

DEPRESSION

It's all over now. For you. Over for good. Over for bad.

You've had your last chance.

You are at bottom.

Even you.

For bad?

The last of an undying breed.

And you blew it. Boy, how you bombed!

What was that?

You actually pretended you knew about computers, informatics.

Blew it!

You said you loved classical music.

You pretended.

There will be no more.

That was the last one. It's over now.

And on top of that your television is broken.

You won't get another.

Every single thing has its price. Every single thing comes at a cost.

Why pay for what you don't use?

Why pay their price?

To begin with you were never very smart. Be honest.

All children, though, have hopes and dreams. Don't they? They are born that way.

You wanted to be a great artist once.

Childlike, they are born with the *capacity* for language and dreaming.

Impersonate.

Four.

Artists drink a lot. You drink a lot.

Vodka costs money.

Artists are smart.

You *overestimated* yourself.

He asked—the interviewer—head down, reading, he asked whether you'd improved your skillset since your last position.

Six syllables. Better. Though it is a compound word, isn't it? Compound, not complex. Sentences. Aren't most?

The one and only job, you mean, you wanted to say.

Are there dumb artists?

Everyone's smarter than you. They all know more.

No more refreshing, nothing to wait on.

They can't be better pretenders. All that practice.

Soon the telephone company will shut off your phone. And the laptop screen will go dark.

You went to the opera once. Even all dressed up and itchy you nearly fell asleep. And then you raved about it afterward: the opera, not nearly falling asleep, not being itchy.

You botched every single answer. Every. Single. One. And you smiled too much. A crooked smile. Like an idiot. You were nervous.

It will be dead. It will not vibrate and turn. It will not ring.

You've never made fun of yourself in front of others. Self-something.

Not even Chris calls anymore.

Seeking advantage you have been mean.

How could you not be nervous? It was your last chance.

Win big with Online Poker and Roulette! Thousands of winners every hour. All credit cards accepted! $50 free credit for new accounts! Play now! Win now!

You almost begged the poor man to hire you out of pity. Kindness? Desperation?

Your parents, for the time being, continue to leave long, quiet, sad messages. They are worried. Once a week you listen to the messages. They alternate who talks. One week it is your dad. The next week it is your mother.

You listen. You never pick up.

The messages are no more than feeble whispers, frightened prayers. Are they embarrassed? Sickened?

For many years you practiced crosswords so you could show off, so others would think you were smart. Smarter. Smarted.

There is a thin volume button on the phone.

The shame you feel. And others. Are your mom and dad ashamed of you?

You barely register.

Communication breakdown.

You are too thin. Gaunt is the word a smart person would use.

Communication has five syllables. Where's the stress?

There's probably a better word.

Look it up.

Objectively, you are not attractive. Far from it.

You barely matter.

You log on.

And you are getting uglier.

A chubby, red button. Both on and off.

Some people are born with taste. Others are not. You were not.

A smart person would know this without having to look it up.

Know how to act.

Can one really acquire taste?

Why log off? One button.

It is a pretentious question.

You have a face for radio, they—your parents'

generation—used to say. CB radio.

Pretentious looks like it should have more syllables than it does. Could there be other pronunciations?

You read books you didn't like.

Five.

Why? You display them, like a phony imitation peacock. All the eyes. First person.

Syllables, not books. You've read more than five books you didn't like. Many more. Honest.

A peahen has little to display. Is it peahen?

Test your IQ. All it takes is five minutes. See how you measure up against friends, coworkers and the rich and famous. Absolutely free!

You do not join in. Participate.

You'll never be what you once were, whatever that was.

Chat is French for cat. Sh.

You'll never be what you were going to be. Not anymore.

French is kind of like Latin. You don't know why. You don't know either.

Most of your stupid online accounts have lapsed, expired.

Gaunt. Hasten your demise.

You failed to keep them active.

That isn't you. Shakespeare? That doesn't sound like you.

Dormant. Dormancy.

You will always be a pretender, a poser. A loser.

Romance.

End it. Kill yourself. Be done with it. End it all.

That sounds more like you.

You are not smart enough to be afraid.

Not something you read.

Your unique personal horoscope reveals your true secret destiny! Free trial today! Unlock the potential of your star chart! Unleash the mysterious powers of the universe!

You are too weak, too tired, and too cowardly.

Were you always a fraud?

Your future is gone. It was ripped from your fingers at the very end, in the eleventh hour.

A-fraid.

You will earn no more money. Ever. Your bank balance will forever go one way.

There are twenty-four hours in every day. Plus some tiny fraction of a second, you think.

Down.

What did you actually possess?

You sleep through most of them, sixteen of twenty-four, maybe less, maybe more. More than eleven.

Your dreams will never ever come true.

You wallow with the other oinkers in the deep troughs of the Internet.

There is no letter f involved. Just the sound of f. Like laugh. Funny.

You were always too weak to push them aside.

You listen to them snort and squeal. Whining swine.

You have no taste.

You have two new messages! Someone is searching for you! See who! Click here!

Slop. You are sloppy.

They—the slick, savvy, suited advertisers, the marketers, the branders—hope the constant blinking will make you click.

Twenty-two years with the same company, climbing the ladder. The one company, the only company, the one and only company.

You blinked. And the ceiling.

Impressive? Old school in a new world.

100

The years you lost.

It doesn't make you feel any better. It doesn't make you feel any worse though. No f sound there.

One job. Your life. Your one and only life.

How could you feel worse?

It is worse than physical pain. It is a pain without location.

Vodka.

The same glass building on the same asphalt street in the same concrete city for twenty-two years. Rain or shine, pain or no.

When was the last time you cleaned the shower?

You shattered your leg once pretending to ski. Couldn't stop.

You think you hear the hairline cracks crawling. Upward.

Snow white cast and sympathy.

Misery loves a chat room.

There must be mice in the walls. Rats maybe.

You used to have a favorite brand. It was named after a classical composer. Now you'll drink anything.

They eat the insulation.

You were never special.

Look behind the Beardsleys. Don't be a-fraid.

You never understood style.

You stand up and bump against the bookcase. The ceramic owl falls. It doesn't break but tiny fractures appear across its back.

Your friends were really not your friends.

Thousands of them.

You'll never log off.

All over the dun painted wings.

You pretended to. Too.

Would it be better if you were able to reach out and touch the person through the screen?

The web commercials are louder and shorter but somehow sadder, more depressing. Their message is muted, fading, like the Beardsleys.

Would that help?

They—them—monitor what you monitor on your monitor.

You wish you could cry. But you are past that. You are dry. Dessicated.

There's a scaly animal called the monitor lizard. Nothing holds your attention.

Only four. How do you know that word?

The future belongs to others. To the children. To your parents.

Everything is stupid.

Like the creeping cracks in the walls.

Paint cracks and peels. Walls crack and crumble. And we all fall down.

The mail piles up by the door.

Walls fall.

You wanted to be a great artist.

You kick it to the side.

Now you are suffering. Now you are drinking. It is too late now.

One day you'll throw it all away without looking at it.

Hard to believe that your life is over but here you are.

At some point you must have talked a good game. Or was it all just luck? Timing? And then your luck ran out.

It's like you're living in a cave, dark and dank.

You were a hard worker. At times. They can't take that away.

No one asks to be born.

Again? Your parents are very religious. They pray for you.

Imagine.

A prison cell.

When was the last time you had a shower?

You told him you'd take anything, do anything. It was not an interview, it was an ambush. It was a setup. It was a trap.

Do pigeons build nests?

No chance.

A good cry won't change matters. A bad cry wouldn't either.

They are too lazy. You are too lazy.

Sentenced to life, whatever that means.

You could be almost anyone, anywhere: lurking, scrolling, watching, reading, waiting, plotting.

They couldn't wait to get you out of there. Out through the revolving doors. Out of their sight. Away from their precious company.

For what?

You have nothing to add.

Citizens of the Internet are called netizens.

You log on and log off. On and off.

The television still doesn't work. Do they have tubes? Too thin.

You wonder whether anyone you know—knew—is on, hiding online.

You survive on corn flakes and white bread bologna sandwiches. You drink vodka and tap water.

Telezens. That is even worse.

Former friendships faded fast. *Alliteration*.

Same. All cold. Refrigeration.

Five syllables.

Answering your parents has made it worse. You call them late at night, when you know that they are asleep and tell them everything is fine. It gives them false hope. It is a necessary cruelty.

From bad to worse.

106

You are a poser.

And it pains you too.

Why do you continue?

Hot singles in your area want to hook up!

You've ruined more than just your own life. They had dreams too. Have.

For how long?

Your dreams will never ever come true.

The past is gone, the future will never arrive.

Worthlessness.

The cracks crackle. The floor groans. The ceiling sags. The owl is mad.

The world is closing in and passing you by, flying by.

Outside, past the window glass, pigeons are multiplying, breeding.

That makes no sense.

The television remote takes up space on the coffee table. You haven't touched it in weeks. It is hidden among unwashed cereal bowls and holey socks.

Fucking pigeons.

It's a metaphor.

You should have done something different with your life? Differently?

That's not who you are.

You thought you were worth more. You thought you were special.

You thought they were the losers. Others.

Who are you?

Netizens. Posters. Social Mediacs. Trolls.

It's a pity party. And you are the guest of honor, the only guest. The only child. Host and guest in the same soiled clothes.

Work was never *the* answer. Was it?

The remote works but the television does not.

What was the question?

Table for one?

A metaphor. A comparison.

You wasted it. Whatever you were given you wasted. All children are born with something, a talent, a future, hopes and dreams.

Parents make things worse.

You'll never get another chance. You blew it.

What are they thinking?

You never get a second chance to make a first impression.

You are lower now than they, smaller.

They are trying at least. They are still trying. Networking. Posting. Talking. Sharing. Chatting. Hoping.

Doing.

Citizens of the Internet Unite!

You are worth less. Worthless.

Poser.

Whatever you had, you wasted.

And for what?

You scroll and mock and see them flirt and fight. Nice or nasty. Sometimes both at once. It is your sad entertainment.

The television is broken. Is it a metaphor?

The only outlet.

You were going to retire to someplace warm.

Be honest with yourself. Finally. There is nothing left to do.

It's not fun, though.

Somewhere you could relax and stop pretending. Could you? Would you?

You should never have been born. You never

asked to be born. You never asked.

Drink in the sun beside a pool.

Imagine.

What will the files say? What will be left?

Arizona.

What was the point?

Florida.

What good follows depression?

You pretended it would be the south of France or Greece.

No posing. Not anymore.

What follows?

There are always two paths.

At least.

An out.

A LADY

Jonathon Swift died in 1745. According to publication records over eighty percent of all novels published in Britain between 1750 and 1790 were published anonymously. Literary anonymity was one of the fashions of the time as the new, not-yet-fully-trusted art form was slowly finding its footing. Novelistic anonymity continued well into the next century.

Even literary reviews—typically penned, it must be admitted, by fellow anonymous novelists—were published unsigned. Reviews were infrequent in the early years of the nineteenth century. For instance, during her lifetime, Jane Austen's novels received but a handful. Those she did receive, however, were generally positive, even glowing. Sir Walter Scott conceded that *there is a truth of painting in her writings which always delights me.* Whereas writer Richard Whately—anonymously, of course—compared Austen favorably to poetic titans like Homer and Shakespeare. Later, George Eliot—another pseudonym—called Austen *the greatest artist that has ever lived.*

Jane Austen was both an innovator and a by-product of her cultural environment. Her deft employment of irony, her piercing commentary, and her powers of observation make her work—apart from being great story-telling—a forerunner to realism. Her descriptions of eighteenth-century landed gentry social life and mores are unsurpassed. Her place in English literature is secure. This is not to say she did not have her critics. Praise for Jane Austen is not universal. Her work was disliked by both Mark Twain and Charlotte Bronte. Her detractors, though, are few. Her fans are legion.

In her lifetime Jane Austen saw four of her novels go to print. She wrote for money. Writing was her livelihood. It was her necessity. It was her passion. But her name, the name Jane Austen, never appeared on her covers. She never took public credit for her work.

Sense and Sensibility (1811) was, per its title page, written "By a Lady." Our Lady—herself clearly a member of the landed gentry—offers as her debut the story of the Dashwood sisters, Elinor (Sense) and Marianne (Sensibility), who suffer the vagaries of love, romance, heartbreak, and disinheritance. The work is a sustained examination of the effects of primogeniture on women of marrying age and the psychological balance necessary to find true happiness. Needing the money, Austen sold the rights for a pittance.

Pride and Prejudice (1813) was penned "By the Author of *Sense and Sensibility.*" *Pride and Prejudice* is an ironic novel of manners pitting Elizabeth Bennet against Mr. Darcy in a romantic battle. Like its predecessor, the novel is set during the British Regency and explores education, marriage, and money, but, most importantly, the necessity of marrying for love, despite social pressures to the contrary. Wealth and social standing alone are not enough to guarantee happiness. Self-knowledge is paramount. The book was wildly successful.

Mansfield Park (1814) was written "By the Author of *Sense and Sensibility* and *Pride and Prejudice*." In this satirical story Fanny Price is sent to live with her wealthy aunt and uncle. The book is a study of meritocracy. It ends in a happy marriage as do almost all of Austen's works, but *Mansfield Park* is in other ways an outlier. It is a symbolic piece of fiction, different from her previous novels. It was—and has remained—controversial for its casual mention of the British slave trade. Despite the difficulties of this work, Austen earned more money from *Mansfield Park* than any of her other books.

Emma (1815) was written "By the Author of *Pride and Prejudice*." Emma Woodhouse and her youthful hubris were dear to Austen. There is an element of autobiography here. *Emma* is a character study within another depiction of the concerns and difficulties facing genteel women in Regency England. To be honest, nothing much happens in the book. There is little action or incident. There is little tension. Emma, unlike Austen's previous heroines, is self-sufficient; she feels no pressure to marry. And yet, in the end, marry she does. Reading *Emma* you get the feeling that this was Austen's favorite work.

During her relatively short life—she died at the

age of forty-one—Jane Austen moved infrequently within a smallish privileged circle, providing her with all the material she would need. Her milieu was her material and her material was her milieu. Largely home-schooled by her brother and father—Austen had but two years total of formal education—she began writing stories at a very young age. Upon publication her books were immediately popular and all of them underwent multiple printings. Austen never wed. What we know about her comes mainly from her books and the anecdotes of others. Although a prodigious letter writer, only 160 of the estimated 3,000 letters in her hand survive.

So, did Austen write anonymously simply because it was the fashion? In part, to be sure. Understanding and interpreting social pressures through novels is different than challenging these forces in reality. But this is only a piece of the answer. It is more likely that gender influenced the decision more than fashion. She was, after all, an eighteenth-century woman. And, in 1811, publicity of any sort was seen as unfeminine, déclassé. Public interest reflected poorly on a woman, especially on a lady of a certain standing. Like the strict separation of classes, English women of the time had their station. No woman should therefore overestimate herself. (It is an irony straight from one of her novels.)

In addition it is also probable that her name would have exposed her small, connected circle of friends and acquaintances as the source material for her works—particularly given her natural ear for speech and dialogue. The fallout would have been socially disastrous, scandalous. She would have been ridiculed, ostracized, and shunned. Literary anonymity was preservation for Austen. And while she lived, no one but her family knew her secret.

Jane Austen died in 1817 from either Addison's disease or Hodgkin's lymphoma, current medical opinions differ. In either case it is a bad way to die. Toward the end of her days she was living *chiefly on the sofa*, gaunt and greatly suffering. She had difficulty walking, lacked energy and was eventually confined to bed. The pain was unbearable, excruciating. She welcomed death. Mercifully she did not have to wait long. After her passing the body was interred in nearby Winchester Cathedral. There it rests still. The words of the epitaph composed by her brother, James, express hope for her salvation, but, significantly, make no mention of her achievements as a writer.

Austen's two other major novels, *Northanger Abbey* and *Persuasion*, were published under her real name following her death. She was not present to raise an objection. She did not have a choice in the matter. Those closest to her must have felt that she no longer required the protection anonymity had provided. Ultimately, perhaps, they were right; the deceased require no protection. Sooner or later, without any assistance from the living, the dead find anonymity.

Twenty years after the burial her six novels were largely forgotten, as if they'd been placed in the ground with her. It wasn't until her nephew published his *A Memoir of Jane Austen* in 1869 that her work was rediscovered and their value recognized. Her major books are still incredibly popular. Her visage appears on the British £10 note. Today, in a world far removed from her era, she is a touchstone for feminists, realists, and writers of all stripes. In her time, as the eighteenth century became the nineteenth, she was an English lady of a certain class who happened to write novels better than anyone else, anonymously. It was her out. It was her escape.

ACCEPTANCE

The end is near.

The end is here. Hear the end. Is.

And you are tired.

The weight of living has lifted and the stage door has opened.

So very tired.

This fog of a life has gone on long enough.

There was a time when a younger you would have said the end is nigh rather than the end is near.

At long last. So tired.

The laptop rests on your lap and you stare at its glow.

You will fight no more.

Like the name says.

You would have said it in a solemn tone faking a smoker's rasp.

You are too tired to tap. You gape at whatever appears on the monitor, whatever page pops up.

The pretense is over.

Nothing is random and everything is random.

You are too tired for tap or touch, mouse or screen. And you never ever got around to setting it up for voice commands. It is now too late for that. You are too tired.

Pretense is past.

Even your voice is worn out. From rasping.

The mourning is over.

Your chapped lips are parted as if about to speak.

And you nap. You sleep.

All the time.

It might be morning. It might be night. It might be dark. It might be light.

But you have nothing left to say to anyone.

Like a baby.

Past tense.

No one checks on you. There are no more messages. This is as it should be.

It might.

The self is all after all.

You were neighbors for long.

Be. Being. Been.

This room. This body. These walls.

This is what lies (lays?) beyond depression. But it no longer matters.

Other things. Other people.

You think less.

Nouns doing verbs.

Unchartered territory.

You are neither depressed nor angry about your

state, your fate.

It is what it is.

Thinking without words is not thought.

The fate of all living beings.

You, an old laptop and the end.

Knowledge, whatever that used to mean, does not matter.

You turn your head and gawk at the skewed Beardsleys on the wrinkled walls. All you see are lines, nonsensical swirling, turning lines.

The quiet expectation of whatever.

And shades. Shading.

Of what comes next.

You never knew much about Zen, but this is not Zen.

Former beings.

Thinking in colors and shapes. Like a child.

It cannot be.

Critical thinking.

Movement catches your eye: the blinking screen, your bony forearm, a droning housefly.

It is barely being.

Lighter here and darker there. Shades. Shading. Shaded.

Peaceful.

Shady.

All more alive than you.

Never been.

To be at peace does not mean that you are happy. There's a difference.

You were, are, and always will be a never was.

Thinking less and less. Speaking hardly at all.

You are full of peace. But you are not happy.

You do not read the back-lit words anymore. They have lost their meaning. They have lost their power.

You curl your toes then let them rise up and stretch toward the faraway ceiling.

Termination.

Movement.

They stand at attention.

Everything ends in *termination*.

You are tired and weak.

And you are waiting.

You don't count anymore.

You sleep often, in short restless spurts; your eyelids are always heavy.

You are done wanting. You are done counting.

You are like a newborn.

Your eyes are moist.

Done taking stock.

And there is no more pretending.

No more crocodile tears.

You scrape yellowy-green chunks of sleep from the inner corners of your watery eyes.

You don't have the strength.

You no longer count.

Often you'll leave the grains until they fall from their own mass, their trivial weight pulled by gravity.

You can surrender without giving up.

The yellowy-green nuggets. The syllables. The words. The thoughts. Fall.

The end is about a void of feelings.

An abyss.

Greens yellow. Browns blacken.

You are not giving up.

Black means death. Red means stop.

You wish a final rest before your long journey.

Oblivion is black.

You are not happy.

And your parents will need help.

The abyss is black. Or white.

A gray empty calm.

You can't help them.

A short journey?

All the colors. None.

Coping.

The dark circle shrinks.

You do not need help.

You avoid feeling.

No bigger. No longer.

They did their best. They fed you. They clothed you. They loved you. Love.

No longer.

You wish to be left alone now.

It is not a decision. It is who you are, what you have become.

Be careful what you wish for.

Resignation.

You drool from your open mouth and drag a dirty sleeve across your chin.

The dark room is a part of you.

Or you allow the saliva to drip to your chest.

You should clean yourself up.

Unrelenting gravity.

It is the last stage.

The gravity of the situation.

Have some dignity.

You talk less and less. Even to yourself.

It is a wordless stage, not a phase. It is a silent performance.

You are part of the room.

Your only authentic performance. Being yourself.

A gesture says more than a noisy word.

Be. Being. Been.

A stick of ordinary furniture to be planted here or there.

Meaning was always beyond you.

To go with peace and dignity, you read once, somewhere. That is the goal.

Meaning is beyond.

Termination.

In your wordless mind you return to a time where nothing was asked of you and all that you wanted was given.

And the self is all.

And there will be no salvation.

And meaning is beyond.

And the couch is your coffin.

You stare. And you blink.

Resignation.

You are again like a child. The circle of life is closing, will close.

There is no lid. Not yet.

Same.

But you lasted longer than the others, longer than you had a right to.

No top. No cap. To tip.

And you surrender.

To shift the balance.

Long enough.

With peace and dignity.

To rest. In peace.

IDENTITY

A POET AND A PROPHET

The end is an illusion. Yet it is a necessary illusion, an evolutionary metaphysical requirement. Without an end there is no purpose, no progress, and no reason to struggle against inevitable death. Human animals need to believe in endings. We need to believe that they are real, that they dwell nearby, that they will reveal themselves in the impending, ineluctable future. As temporal—and temporary—creatures we demand logical structures. We manufacture them. As young children we are told there was a beginning. So there must be an end. One's *lifetime* becomes orderly, a progression. It is another segment on the continuum. But every person creates their own end(s) according to their own vocabulary. The illusory end is an *other*, an unspoken concept of amorphous contours continually floating in the future of the mind's eye.

The end is always unknown. Ambiguity is the nature of illusion. And this obscurity is why we fear the end, illusion or not. Fear is a powerful motivator. Fear makes us move. Fear makes us flee. Fear makes us seek to hide. Sometimes, some of us—writers, creators, artists, etc.—lean on anonymity in response to this fear.

Siegfried Sassoon (1886-1967) was a noted English poet and a decorated war hero. His daring exploits during World War One made him something of a legend among the British public. He was seemingly fearless. Once, he single-handedly charged a fortified German trench without a thought to his own welfare. (Nor did he plan what to do with the trench once captured. Rather than calling for immediate reinforcements Sassoon sat down in the newly liberated mud and read a book of poetry.) He was rash. Fellow soldiers were bemused. Some saw him as a lucky charm and wanted to be near him. Others considered him suicidal and kept their distance. By all accounts Siegfried Sassoon, facing the life and death horrors of *the war to end all wars*, had never once shown the slightest hint of being afraid. Of anything.

Born to a Jewish father and an Anglo-Catholic mother, Sassoon grew up in a country mansion amid servants and luxury. His father was a member of the wealthy Baghdadi Sassoon family, international merchants, and, although disinherited from the family business for marrying outside the faith, remained rich. His mother was a member of the Thornycrofts, the same Thornycrofts responsible for many of the more famous statues populating the city of London. Sassoon wanted for nothing. His parents separated when he was four.

Sassoon's sexual relationships were mainly homosexual (he would later marry) and he was a very good cricket player, though in his youth he never quite managed to make the formidable Kent squad.

After Cambridge, Sassoon left the opulence of genteel Kent with a small private fortune, sufficient to live on modestly without troubling about employment.

He moved to London where in 1913 he published his first successful work *The Daffodil Murders,* a parody of Masefield.

Motivated by patriotism he volunteered for armed service just before the outbreak of the war. The Western Front was hell on earth and combat quickly changed Sassoon's beliefs and his poetry. His verse, heretofore suffused with Romanticism, became bleak and realistic, full of rotting corpses, sticky black blood and mangled limbs. *No truth unfitting* was his motto. In unflinching language he described the horrors of the trenches and satirized the jingoistic pretensions of those responsible. His new poetry was the poetry of Modernism. Increasingly reckless on the battlefield, Sassoon volunteered for night raids and bombing patrols earning him the dubious nickname *Mad Jack.*

His temerity grew alongside an intensifying hatred of the war. And, after being granted R&R and sent back to England, he fell in with Bertrand Russell among others and became a vocal dissenter, refusing to return to the front. In a lone protest in 1917 Sassoon sent a soldier's declaration to his superiors and the press earning him enmity and infamy. Out of frustration and anger—for a number of reasons, including the recent death of a good friend—he also threw the ribbon of his military cross into the Mersey. Here was a uniformed soldier blatantly and publicly disobeying his commanders. His actions did not go unnoticed.

However, thanks to his well-documented bravery—and, perhaps family connections—he was spared a certain court-martial. Instead, authorities ordered him to a military psychiatric hospital to recover from an *obvious case of shell shock*. While in the hospital he met and greatly influenced poet and fellow soldier Wilfred Owen. Owen learned a great deal about the poetic arts from the older Sassoon during their brief friendship. (Owen returned to the battlefield only to die in the waning months of the war. He would posthumously emerge as the greatest of the war poets, eclipsing even his mentor.)

After his mandated psychiatric stay, Sassoon was returned to service visiting relatively peaceful Palestine before rejoining the war on the Western Front where he was promptly shot in the head by friendly fire. Fortunately he survived the injury, but his fighting days were over. The war soon ended.

For a while, following his discharge, he dabbled in politics before joining the left-wing *Daily Herald* as its literary editor.

Nine years after the Treaty of Versailles Sassoon was adding the finishing touches to a completely new work and he was afraid. He was afraid his new literary effort—a humorous autobiographical piece of prose fiction—wasn't any good. In fact he was afraid it was horrid. And he had good reason to doubt its success. He was a dark modernist war poet turning to light humor. It was a radical departure. He was afraid of being mocked. He feared ridicule.

Memoirs of a Fox-Hunting Man (1928) was published anonymously, its author a mystery. Mad Jack was too afraid to claim authorship. Fear can be a strong motivator.

The novel examines the sanguine youth of George Sherston, Sassoon by another name. Fox hunting represents pre-war innocence. The book is a charming and witty coming-of-age tale. It became an instant classic. Relieved, Sassoon went on to complete the Sherston trilogy—attaching his name to the second and third volumes—and his literary fame was assured.

Toward the end of his long life Sassoon converted to Catholicism. After all he had done and seen and survived he opted to accept Jesus Christ as man and God and looked forward to the promised eternal peace of biblical heaven. That, he believed, would be his end. Sassoon died of stomach cancer at the age of eighty, less than one week before his eighty-first birthday, undoubtedly unafraid of what lay ahead.

Eric Blair assumed the pen name George Orwell because he didn't want to embarrass his *lower-upper-middle class* family. (He was concerned his years of tramping among the downtrodden would reflect poorly on them. He was afraid of hurting them.) In addition, thought Blair, the name has the sound *of a good round English name*. That was how he saw it.

Blair was born in British India and taken to

England when he was one. His great-grandfather, Charles Blair, had been a wealthy country gentleman who had increased his fortune by marrying the daughter of the Earl of Westmoreland. She entered the marriage with her own income as the absentee landlord of several Jamaican plantations (see *Mansfield Park*). But Eric Blair was not born into money. His father was a mere civil servant; family prosperity was in its past.

In England Blair managed to obtain a scholarship seat at Eton though he was an indifferent student. And rather than follow his peers to Oxford or Cambridge he became a member of the Imperial Police and chose a posting in Burma.

While in Burma he was known as an outsider. He became fluent in Burmese and acquired circular tribal tattoos on each knuckle. According to Karen tribal lore, the tattoos are meant to protect against bullets and snake bites.

In 1927 Blair contracted dengue fever and was returned to England to convalesce. During this hiatus he quit the police and decided to become a writer. On and off for the next six years, gathering material for a book, Blair bummed around London and Paris living as an indigent and working menial jobs under the guise of itinerant P.S. Burton. Blair became obsessed with poverty and economic injustice and in 1933 *Down and Out in Paris and London* was published to moderate success. And Eric Blair became George Orwell.

Orwell published more frequently after his first novel was released, writing hundreds of reviews. In 1936 he married and, in a car driven by Henry Miller, sped to Spain to fight the fascists. Orwell was a tall man—he stood over six feet two inches—and the Spanish repeatedly warned him to keep his head down. Despite their insistent warnings he was shot in the throat by a sniper. He survived and returned to England. The tattoos had, perhaps, worked their magic. In 1937, as he was recovering from his wound, he contracted a case of tuberculosis.

Orwell was deemed unfit for military service when World War Two erupted. His wife got work at the Censorship Department while he wrote for the *Partisan Review* and the *Observer*. In 1941 he joined the BBC and became literary editor at the *Tribune*.

Lucid prose and common-sense leftism made Orwell a highly sought-after commodity during the war. And while he was writing for others he began work on an anti-Stalin tale that he said would be *a fusion of political purpose and artistic purpose into a whole.*

Animal Farm (1945) was an immediate international success. The satirical work pits farm animal against farmer. Half fable and half allegory, the novella has never been out of print. Among other lessons, the story teaches that man exploits animals in much the same way as the rich exploit the poor. The latent powers of the animals and of the poor remain unrealized. Had Orwell written nothing else, *Animal*

Farm would have guaranteed him a permanent place in the literary canon. *All animals are equal.*

Eric Blair as George Orwell was now famous. Pseudonymity no longer mattered. He had traded one name for another. There was no hiding.

In 1947 tuberculosis returned and never released its deadly grip. Illness and impending death, however, did not prevent him from writing his masterpiece and best-known work, *Nineteen Eighty-Four* (1949).

The dystopian novel envisions an upside-down world of perpetual war and omnipresent government surveillance in which *War is Peace, Freedom is Slavery,* and *Ignorance is Strength.* Individualism and independent thinking are persecuted. The proletariat is kept sedated with alcohol, pornography, and a national lottery—which, predictably, is never paid out. We now refer to such as totalitarian society as Orwellian.

In the novel Winston Smith works for the government—Big Brother is the omnipresent embodiment of the all-powerful party—rewriting past newspaper articles to support party lines. The original documents are then destroyed by fire in a *memory hole.* Smith leads a poor, disaffected life struggling to believe in the benevolence and truth allegedly underpinning Big Brother. He correctly assumes it is only a matter of time before the thought police arrive and *vaporize* him for his unpatriotic, indeed treasonous, ruminations. (The vigilant, ever-present thought police are a shadowy force responsible for the removal and *disappearance* of ordinary men and women, erasing all traces of their existence.) Party punishment goes beyond mere assassination, beyond anonymity; it is as if one had never been born. You are there and then you never were. In the story Smith falls in love with a coworker but betrays her and independent thought when caught, tortured, reeducated, and, finally, confronted with his worst fear: rats. The book closes as Smith admits his love for Big Brother. There is nothing more to say. The end.

Nineteen Eight-Four introduced us to a number of phrases and ideas that have become part of our political and cultural zeitgeist: cold war, Big Brother, Thought Police, newspeak, doublespeak, thought crime, and others.

Both *Nineteen Eighty-Four* and *Animal Farm* share the idea of the betrayed revolution and one's subordination to the collective, to enforced class divisions, and to the cult of personality. Orwell presciently recognized man's instinctual base desire to brutalize and subjugate his fellow man in the name of absolute power. He predicted the sordid state of the world well before his vision became frightening reality.

He never lived to see the fulfillment of his prophecies by Stalin and others. He never beheld the evils he foretold. At the age of forty-six an artery in one of Orwell's lungs burst killing him.

A poet and a prophet: one a homosexual, the

other a homophobe. Both shaped by the horrors of war and man's injustice to man, both seeking the protection of anonymity.

Siegfried Sassoon, war hero, poet and humorist, was anonymous inwardly, privately, personally. Orwell, the reformer, prophet and novelist, was pseudonymous outwardly, publicly, politically. Sassoon's anonymity was a sensitive hiccup, a temporary artistic blip. Eric Blair was completely and utterly effaced by George Orwell. Anonymity may not last after all. It is not always the way things end. Opposites may complement.

War is Peace. Freedom is Slavery. Ignorance is Strength.

Anonymity is identification.

REBIRTH

But it is not the end. It is not so easy. Not for you. One door closes. Is there another? Another beginning? Stuck in the middle? Not the end. Not for you. Yet.

You are confused.

You are mad.

You awake to a new world. And you are new. Again.

You woke. You thought it was over. You hoped. It had been over.

Is awake the right word? Renewed. Naked again. Similar but not the same.

You are always wrong. Stupid.

You are not tired.

But you are hungry. Starving. Angry and hungry.

An empty bottle falls to the floor as you rise. A blanket binds your legs. You kick free. You step to the window. You raise the blinds. It must be late morning.

You are wrong, as usual. Mourning never ends. The time of day or night makes no difference. Not to you. Not anymore.

You turn on the lights, one by one. The trumpet lamp still without a bulb. You vow to pick one up when you go out.

Why bother?

You are going to go out. You will go out. Outside. Out of doors.

You'll only get hurt. Again. By others. Yourself.

The Beardsleys are straight. The cracks fainter, fewer.

But they haven't gone away. They're still there.

You clean.

You're filthy.

You shower.

You're all wet. Sweating. Soaked.

You get dressed. And you put on clean clothing.

144

Nothing fits. It hangs. They've never fit.

You will go out.

Don't.

You tell yourself—for no other reason than the fact that you are still alive—that this is the first day of a new you. The end was not the end after all. You take a deep breath. You were mistaken. You try to convince yourself that everything is not over.

The pain will return. You will bring it back. Worse this time. You cough.

You are unsteady—uncertain—and yet you move. Forward.

You always were unsure, lurching. You always moved without a purpose. Danced for others.

One day and then the next. And another. One following the other.

You're letting the feelings back in. It is wrong. It is unwise.

You develop a routine.

A boring false existence.

You recreate a life. You shape it. Like a sculpture. It feels a lot like pretending, but you live like you have a life.

Finally, something you're halfway decent at—pretending. A new you back to old tricks.

You eat right. Balanced. You have the food—most of it anyway—delivered to your door. You make the arrangements online. Everything is done online. The world is online.

It tastes like sewage, colorless, inedible. Bland boiled vegetables, soggy pasta. The food tastes like it is online, empty and artificial.

You develop interests. You explore. Online.

Ah, your only friend the laptop. You hug it tightly, afraid to let go.

It is the way of the new world.

It is not your way. It is not your world. You are not welcome.

You see your parents. You talk. FaceTime. Skype.

Every weekend. They look happy to see you.

They look so old. They won't be around much longer. They are dying. You see it.

They sit close, side by side, no gap, on a beige leather couch you recognize. Sometimes they tap the wrong button on the screen and you are met with your own face, huge now, staring back at you. Confused.

Ugly as ever. Not a new you.

Another tap and they return, apologizing.

Not for long. Their end is near. You will again be alone.

You feel like it's your fault. They blame *the machine*.

It is your fault. It is *all* your fault. You ruined their lives and yours.

You shower every morning at eight a.m. You wash and condition your hair. You slide your soapy fingers between your toes. Scrub. Fifteen to seventeen minutes.

Why do you bother? No one looks at you. No

one sees you.

You make amends with Chris. You text each other. Every day. At least. You are friends again.

Yes, you crawled back. You ate crow. You apologized. You begged.

You have a friend, again. You are not alone.

But you are alone, aren't you? Chris is not really your friend. More pretending.

Two hours a day, usually in the late afternoon, you play a game called *Minescraper*. Online. Chris plays too. You message while you're playing. You work as a team. Explore together.

And further pretending. No wonder you like playing. It's just a game. Or is it? You're afraid to ask yourself if it's more than a game, aren't you?

Sometimes you smile for no reason.

You are afraid of yourself, aren't you? Who isn't?

Your parents wire money into your bank account every week. It is more than enough.

You are a child, dependent on others for survival. You are good at saying thank you, well-practiced.

During your black morning coffee and your moon-shaped croissant you read the day's news. Umber flakes fall from your food and land on the keyboard. You keep up with the current events. There is always something happening in the world. It keeps turning. It never stops. Breakfast lasts approximately one hour.

One hour to read about real people doing real things, real events happening while you clean and shower, while you play your electronic games, while you pretend to live.

Two hours in the morning and two hours in the afternoon you network on three different social media sites. It is a promise you made to your parents. You have conversations and information exchanges with others. Nobody admits they're looking for work, but everybody knows.

What a joke! No one will ever hire you. You will never work again. You will never be a functional part of society. You've been down this road. It is all for show. Four hours a day just so you can lie to your poor paying parents. Four hours penance.

In exchange for the money they give you.

Their hard-earned money.

For ninety minutes every day you visit museum websites and look at the art. You stare and wonder and lose yourself in the paintings and sculptures. This is for you.

More play. More selfishness.

You sometimes comment on the artwork or comment on the comments to the artwork.

To criticize, right? To mock? As if you could do any better? As if your opinions are worth anything. What do you know?

You consider picking up your brushes again. You were going to be an artist.

And you failed. Sure, go ahead, fail again.

You find a great website that helps increase vocabulary.

Still trying to better yourself? Why?

A mediocre artist is still an artist, you figure.

Is a bad artist still an artist? Even mediocrity is beyond your reach.

You stop counting syllables—vocabulary is not measured in syllables—but you try to learn a new word every single day. The word-a-day application pronounces the word for you, correctly, slowly.

You will forget them. You will misuse them. You will mispronounce them, one by one, embarrassing yourself.

Augmented reality was the first. Two words really. One you know. Knew.

Did you?

You scour the bathroom thoroughly twice a week. You polish the shower tiles. You clean the grout.

Maybe you could network yourself into a job cleaning rest stop toilettes?

You tell yourself that you will repaint the walls. All the walls. A different color. Colors. Bright. Vibrant.

Then you could call yourself a painter, if not an artist.

Cover the cracks.

And your ego.

And new window treatments.

Why not plastic surgery?

When you have money.

After they're dead, you mean.

Money that doesn't come from your parents. Money that is yours, not a hand out.

A dreamer dreaming a dreamy dream.

The object of *Minescraper* is to create your own little paradise. You walk or run or swim or fly around various landscapes interacting with the environment and other avatars. You build up and you tear-down. You collect valuable resources.

Too many metaphors there.

Chris created an elaborate towering house made of diamonds.

Of course, it shines.

You have a cave on a cliff.

Indecisive as ever. At the top and buried. Stuck in the middle.

You dig and build. And interact. You trade.

You pretend.

Sometimes it rains in *Minescraper*. There are wild animals. Mysterious portals. At night zombies can attack.

You hide. Does Chris protect you?

The days and nights are accelerated.

Sound familiar?

You don't drink as much as you used to.

You miss it, don't you? Vodka. You miss drinking and passing out. You miss the taste and the numb buzz before the black. You were good at something. Dedicated.

You sleep better. You sleep on the sofa bed instead of on cushions. You make the bed every single day. You wash the sheets and pillowcases once a week.

A hotel! You could work in a cheap hotel. Cleaning. Making beds. Fluffing pillows.

The election is coming up. It is the biggest current event, the most talked about, the most commented on. You know the candidates and their positions. You read.

You know what they say, what they want you to think. You know what they want you to know. That's all you know.

You may even vote this time around.

You won't. And, even if you did, it wouldn't matter. Your vote doesn't mean anything. Nothing changes.

You have enough money for art supplies now. Your parents have been generous.

You are stealing their retirement savings. They are sacrificing themselves. So you can buy paint? Expensive brushes?

You have a favorite.

Candidate or parent? Brush?

Kleptocracy is one of the words.

There is no word for what you are doing.

There are hundreds of art forums online. Some are quite good. Kindred spirits, you would have once said.

Bums, you also once said.

Just because a part of your life is over doesn't mean life is over.

Depends at whose expense. Depends who you are hurting.

Unless you *want* your life to be over. That is always an option.

Keep your options open. Sound advice.

You keep moving. You have a routine.

You move to keep moving. Your routine is a crutch. Your new life is a sham, same as the old sham.

Renaissance means rebirth.

Born again. Your stupid parents and their stupid

life-prolonging money.

The artwork of the Renaissance always moves you. Your eyes well. It's almost too good, too perfect.

You'd never be any good. You know better. Not even you are that dumb.

Your parents encourage you to explore the possibilities. They gave you life. They want you to be happy, fulfilled.

Your parents are old and delusional.

Chris comes over sometimes with a bottle of expensive red wine and you talk until it's late. Stories about work no longer hurt.

You've forgotten—already—how much that life meant to you. You feel you're now above it because you think you've survived something intense and meaningful.

You can laugh.

But that's just crap like everything else.

You never replaced your television. You never needed a television in the first place.

Yes, you did. Yes. There were times you needed television more than anything.

You start to sketch. You doodle. Long curving lines on thick creamy paper.

Bird scratches on the page. The cracks on your walls are more artistic.

On one of the websites all you really do is repeat old jokes, bumper sticker humor. Sometimes you come up with jokes of your own. Puns. They are not very funny. But others repeat them anyway. They like them.

They are pretending too. Surely you see that. You are not funny. You never have been. Morose. Isn't that one of your words? See the world through morose colored glasses.

That's the social aspect of it.

The fake part of it, you mean.

Your apartment has never been cleaner or brighter. The view out the spotless window has improved, the skyline renewed. It's like the buildings have shifted around to create a more dramatic cityscape. Inside, your books no longer lean. They stand erect and organized. Even the cracked owl appears happier.

Yes, maybe a hotel. Or a hospital.

Like *Minescraper* played in real life. Build up and tear-down.

You are blurring your worlds. Be careful. It won't end well. It won't end.

The more attention you give someone online the more attention you receive. Like in real life. Tit for tat. That's the way the world works. Networks. Nets work.

And pyramid schemes. Ponzi traps.

The pigeons don't visit your windowsill now that you open the blinds every day. You can still hear them though, nearby, cooing.

Are they speaking to you? Do they coo nature's words of wisdom?

Burbling.

Belching.

The sunlight shines on your possessions. Your oriental rug looks brighter, the blues bluer, the reds more radiant. The vacuumed sofa bed appears to have been reupholstered.

But in reality your stuff is old and worn. The light may brighten, but it does not transform.

The refrigerator emits a happy hum.

A refrigerator packed with tasteless internet food purchased on the backs of your poor parents.

Even inanimate objects do better fulfilling their purpose. The trumpet lamp shines a perfect circle on the ceiling. The squat steel chairs gleam with patient strength.

Unlike you, they have a purpose. They were wanted. They exist for a reason.

You've added three new books to your bookcase. One is a novel you've yet to read by Jane Austen. One is a biography of Picasso. And the third book is some kind of fictional anthropology.

You won't understand them. But you'll be sure to point them out to Chris, won't you?

They were on sale.

Still your parents' money.

Keeping active, busy, improves your outlook. It improves most everything.

Keeps you from thinking.

Human beings were meant to do things. Human beings were designed to move.

Most human beings. Some should never have been born. Some are mistakes.

There are many ways to be active.

You?

You make friends playing *Minescraper*. Real live people behind rectangular avatars message you. Strangers, people who do not know Chris. People from all over the world. Different people. Terry is your favorite.

You are one of the people hiding behind an online character. Hiding does not make you special.

You develop relationships while telling jokes. You learn about other people's lives. They learn about yours.

Do they really?

They learn what you share.

You don't share the good stuff, the real stuff, the pain.

There is no pressure.

Because it's all fake.

It is voluntary, almost natural. It evolves.

Naturally fake, then.

You eat three healthy meals a day. You make sure. You don't snack.

Eat and get fat.

Your parents sometimes send extra.

Money and food.

You don't drink vodka anymore. Just wine. With meals. Usually.

The one thing you did well you've abandoned. Yes, it's a wonderful life.

After breakfast, after reading the news, you walk around the block three times. At first it took twenty-seven minutes, now it takes you twenty-two.

Something to tell your parents. You brag. A way to pretend you're an actual person with a real life.

You are getting faster. Fitter.

To what end?

Chris suggests you join a gym.

You won't.

The Beardsleys hang straight now. Maybe you're walking different. Less pounding. Softer steps.

Maybe the apartment is crooked. Maybe it's your perspective, dummy.

Nights pass in dreamless sleep. Maybe twice a week or so, after midnight, you wake to go to the bathroom. But that's normal.

How old are you really? The age you feel or the number of years you've lived? How you look?

You are educating yourself. Online.

It is not education. It is biding time. You are a phony.

The bathroom smells like Original Scent Febreze.

What else does the fragrance hide?

You tossed the remote control when you dumped the television. You don't miss it, though sometimes you remember the dual-purpose red button.

On or off. Again no middle ground with you or your objects.

Autodidact is one of your new words.

So is impotence.

Your parents are very nice people. You doubt everybody can say that.

You know everybody can't say that. You only say it yourself to lessen your guilt.

You answer the mail as it arrives; most of it is electronic, most of it unimportant.

Like you. Impotent. Barren.

You shower at eight a.m., washing and conditioning your thinning hair, scrubbing between your turning toes. And then you get dressed in clean clothes.

Day in, day out. You are a shiny empty robot.

You never wear anything two days in a row. Your clothes are kept clean.

Mommy and Daddy will buy you new clothes.

It is routine.

It is pointless.

Your friends in *Minescraper*—Terry and others— talk about other online games.

They talk about a lot of things though.

You are curious.

Or bored.

By nature.

And slow and lazy and ugly and untalented and worthless. By nature.

Renaissance. Rebirth.

Again?

A DEEP THROAT

At some unremarkable, unrecorded minute in the second half of the twentieth century we lost the ability to effectuate real anonymity. The era(s) of our collective cultural history when true concealment was desirable, or possessed value, passed unnoticed. Those days are gone forever. For better or worse the world changed technologically and we with it. We may have become too evolved. Or too curious. Too suspicious. We traded privacy for convenience. We swapped freedom for ease. Anonymity — authentic anonymity — no longer confers the long-term benefits and protection it once promised. It no longer makes evolutionary or practical sense. True lasting anonymity has no place in our lightening-paced, camera-laden, interconnected world. Anonymity is an artifact. Only the idea — an ideal — remains. *Temporary* anonymity and pseudo-pseudonymity, then, are our age's answers to personal and public concealment. They are but weak substitutes. At best they are poor placeholders. But the modern era is not equipped to support the realization of total anonymity. We are unable and, more significantly, unwilling to grasp the concept. Anonymity makes us uncomfortable. It makes us restive and wary. Real anonymity — authentic enduring anonymity — is a relic of our past, like cave dwelling or clean air.

But that does not mean we stop trying. It does not mean we've abandoned all attempts. Privacy and secrecy and mystery will always have their allure. Anonymity will always possess appeal. Some of us need to wear the mask, even though we understand its façade of immunity will one day fall away. As a species we will keep playing at anonymity, knowing our attempts are fruitless. We will keep hiding. And sometimes we might experience a period of relative success. Every once in a while we may, for a moment in time, recapture the true spirit of anonymity.

In November 1972 the thirty-seventh President of the United States Richard M. Nixon was reelected with almost sixty-one percent of the popular vote. Less than two years later he would resign in disgrace. In large part his unprecedented fall was due to an anonymous informant.

In addition to Nixon's resignation, executive office crimes resulted in prison terms for White House Chief of Staff H.R. Haldeman, G. Gordon Liddy, White House Counsels Charles Colson and John Dean, former Attorney General John Mitchell, as well as presidential advisor John Erlichman. The scandal that demolished the second Nixon administration was known as Watergate.

Watergate began on June 17, 1972 when five men were apprehended on the sixth floor of the Watergate Hotel in downtown Washington, D.C. The dark-clothed, flashlight-bearing men were caught breaking into the offices of the Democratic National Committee. One of them, James McCord Jr., worked security for

Nixon's committee for reelection. Two of the burglars carried the personal telephone number of White House staffer and former CIA agent Howard Hunt. Two days after the badly botched break-in, an anonymous source assured Bob Woodward—then a young reporter for the *Washington Post*—that it was safe to draw a direct link between the attempted Watergate crime and the Oval Office. This assurance was the beginning of the end for Nixon.

Deep Throat was the catchy sobriquet given to the confidential informant who provided ongoing information to Woodward about the involvement of the Nixon administration in the Watergate scandal. Deep Throat, so dubbed by a *Washington Post* editor, alludes to the deep background status of the source. (It was also the name of a pornographic film popular at the time.) The mysterious source helped narrate the story of the 1972 break-in. He directed the *Post* reporters toward the later revelations of the Nixon administration's campaign of spying and sabotage against perceived enemies. He told Woodward about the president's secret taping system. He hinted at the deliberately erased eighteen and a half minutes of missing recordings. Deep Throat guided the media's investigation.

The nickname was introduced to the general public in the 1974 book *All the President's Men* written by Woodward and his colleague at the *Post*, Carl Bernstein. Two years later the book was turned into an award-winning film starring Robert Redford and Dustin Hoffman. Hal Holbrook played the role of the inscrutable Deep Throat.

Throughout the Watergate investigation Woodward and Deep Throat maintained an elaborate system of signals and secure routines, very cloak and dagger. Allegedly, the reporter signaled Deep Throat by moving a flowerpot with a red flag around the balcony of his apartment. When Deep Throat wished to meet he would, again allegedly, make special markings on page twenty of Woodward's daily copy of the *New York Times*. The two men often met in the early morning hours on the basement level of an underground garage in Rosslyn. In 2011 a historical marker was placed at the entrance to the garage denoting its significance in the presidential scandal.

Deep Throat remained anonymous for over thirty years. His identity was a closely guarded secret. Even Bernstein didn't know. For decades pundits and reporters speculated about the source's real name. Woodward remained mum. It became a political media game of cat and mouse. At one time or another dozens of people were suspected and accused of being *that voice in the garage*, including: Nixon speech writer Pat Buchanan, FBI number two at the time Mark Felt, Secretary of State Henry Kissinger, CIA head William Colby, then-Chief Justice Williams Rehnquist, General Alexander Haig, and even White House staffer turned television journalist Diane Sawyer.

Others firmly believed Deep Throat was invented by the reporters for dramatic purposes or, at best, was a composite character, an amalgam of several well-placed sources. In a later book, *The Secret Man: The Story of Watergate's Deep Throat*, Woodward shrugs off this line of speculation maintaining that Deep Throat was a single individual, a mystery man.

And that's pretty much the way things stayed for thirty years. Then, in 2005, a family attorney identified former FBI Associate Director Mark Felt as Deep Throat. The bombshell was quickly confirmed by Bob Woodward. At the time Felt was ninety-two and suffering from dementia. His life was coming to an end. He would die in 2008.

There are those who contend Nixon knew all along that the informant was Felt. Some maintain the president had no idea who was behind Deep Throat. The former claim the president believed firing Felt would have been worse than a burglary scandal given the information Felt was privy to. Whereas the latter point to supposed evidence that Nixon had ordered FBI Director Gray to fire Felt at least five separate times.

If Felt was Deep Throat, what was his motivation? Was he a hero or traitor? Was he a patriot or an avenger? Could he have been both? Did he disclose classified information out of a sense of morality, believing he was protecting the FBI? Was he trying to insulate the FBI from the meddling Nixon

White House? Did he do it out of patriotism, believing he was revealing the Nixon White House as contemptuous of presidential norms? Was he trying to protect the office of the presidency?

Or did he do it for purely personal reasons? Felt had been passed over to lead the FBI. He was not awarded the directorship he believed he'd earned. And, worse, Acting Director L. Patrick Gray was a bureau outsider. Was the goal to nudge Nixon to name Felt director over the acting director? Did Deep Throat leak highly classified information to demonstrate that Gray couldn't control the bureau, that he was ill-suited for the job?

We will never know the real answer. Perhaps there were many truths. Perhaps it is a question of perspective. In any event Felt took his Deep Throat motives with him to the grave.

We do know, however, that he was no paragon of virtue. Felt was a long-time intelligence insider devoted to the Big Brother Hoover way of operating. He had, among other dubious operations, authorized illegal burglaries as part of the FBI's investigations into leftists, specifically the radical Weather Underground. (In 1980, for his part in the illegal break-ins, Felt was convicted on felony charges. He was pardoned the following year by Ronald Reagan.) Mark Felt was no angel.

Reporters are taught in journalism school that anonymous sources invariably have an axe to grind.

Most leaks are personal. And people usually act in their best interest. Disclosure of sensitive information is often done to boost the leaker's ego or to earn goodwill from reporters for future use. It can also be done to advance particular policy initiatives, to launch trial balloons, or to simply *blow the whistle* on perceived wrongdoings. And information can be leaked anonymously to inflict damage on another party.

There are those who believe that Felt, a seasoned intelligence agent, gamed Woodward and played the *Washington Post*. Were the media—were Woodward and Bernstein—used by a unelected official with a personal agenda? The reporters say no. To this day Woodward believes that Felt was a patriot doing his sworn duty to protect and defend the institutions of a democratic America. He claimed the files, the FBI files—once they were unsealed—would bear this out.

But there was a plot twist when the files were finally made public. The documents failed to match what Woodward was told by Deep Throat. They did not align with the reporter's notes. Felt's tips did not run parallel to the FBI investigation. In fact they were entirely different. So, the question becomes, was Felt such a brilliant counterintelligence agent that he managed to cover his tracks to perfection? Was this even possible? Or is there an easier, more likely, explanation?

For decades—based almost exclusively on Woodward's recollections and reputation—observers and critics presumed that Deep Throat was simply regurgitating the FBI's own investigation of Watergate to the reporter with a slight time delay on the information. And Felt, as FBI number two, was perfectly placed to do so. However, according to the actual FBI files, Deep Throat provided Woodward information that was not part of the larger investigation. Furthermore, Deep Throat produced specifics that almost certainly had to have originated in the White House. If these facts were not in the FBI report they could not have come from Felt.

This discordance has led some to conclude that although Felt might have been Deep Throat, he did not act alone. Felt's privileged information required an accomplice. But this new conclusion was not a return to the Deep Throat as composite theory. No, Deep Throat was most likely, according to this latest, speculative, theory, a duet: one source singing from inside the FBI and one source fiddling from the White House. Felt must have worked with somebody else. And the most logical conspirator in the Nixon White House at the time, according to this theory, was John Dean. *That rat Dean*, Nixon called him. (John Dean worked as White House Counsel to Nixon for almost three years, until April of 1973. He became a key witness for the prosecution during Watergate and fed them information while working in the White House. In his plea deal he accepted guilt on a single felony count.) Dean was present at every crucial Oval Office discussion surrounding Watergate. He knew the secret plans and the secret players. Given such access Dean could not have gone to the media directly. He would have been revealed as the source in short order. And this provided Felt, angry over the direction of the FBI, the perfect cover. Dean coming forward most certainly would have had his motives questioned. His reliability would have been an issue. The media would have been skeptical. Felt was cleaner. One of the good guys.

In all probability, then, Felt and Dean together were Deep Throat. Deep Throat was the production of a duo with Felt as the front man. Felt was the throat. Dean was the deep. And young Bob Woodward had no reason to question the music behind the silvery voice. If this was indeed the case, if John Dean was the informant behind the informant, he managed to achieve almost perfect anonymity.

We may have outlived the golden age of anonymity, but that does not mean people will cease trying. Perhaps Dean has provided us with a final example. Maybe there will be others. Maybe there are more mysteries left. Anonymity will always be attractive. Masks are sexy. And there is always an axe to grind.

REPLAY

You play two online games, seriously. For hours. Every single day, every lighted night.

You used to also play a third game, but you quit. Like a little bitch. But you won't talk about that, will you?

They are serious fun, best part of the day.

Empty diversions, that's what they are, meaningless distractions. It's just you hiding behind a screen, avoiding the real world.

You played a third. But it was too intense and too serious. The people weren't nice. You argued. You were harassed. Disrespected. So you left.

Ah, you did mention it. But of course you lied. You spoke half the truth. You didn't confess to what really happened. You are half of a coward.

Anyway, two games are enough for you, for now. Not enough hours in a day. Nights aren't long enough. Two games are plenty.

The nights are plenty long. You pretend not to be scared. Daytime—the light—lets you forget how dark the nights are. You pretend to be busy. There's a difference.

Clash of Legends is the newest game. It's your favorite. You get to be famous warriors from history: Genghis Khan, Alexander the Great, Joan of Arc. Chris doesn't like it. Terry loves it. Terry was the one who told you about it. You are still learning the ropes, getting better at it.

Terry told you this. Terry told you that. Terry likes it. Do you see a problem here?

A lot about online role-playing games is about interacting, messaging with the other people. The games you play are very social. It's a new way to meet people. It's another way to communicate.

It is a new way to avoid communication, a new way to avoid people. Pretending to be someone else you pretend to talk to other pretenders. It's sad. It smacks of desperation, sad, lonely desperation.

Every game has its own shorthand. The game shapes the language. You need to converse. The messages are brief and funny, usually. Some of the people are really funny. Witty banter.

These gamers you call funny and witty are

society's outcasts. They are the ones who cannot function in the real world, the ones who can't make it on the outside. And you are one of them. But you are neither funny nor witty, are you? You are the lowest of the low.

Being online is more fun and more interesting than anything in your apartment or outside your door. It is bigger and brighter. It's more varied, realer. It is hyperreal, if that's a real word.

You struggle to define what's real and what is not. You always have. It is harder at night, isn't it? Blurrier. Darker.

You really need a new computer with a bigger screen and better graphics. Everyone talks about their system, what they're playing on. Sometimes it's just a phone. Sometimes it's a home theater.

Building a better, safer and less real world through technology.

Like other gamers you start to call the Internet the interwebs. You find the word clever. You picked it up online. Where else?

Interwebs is clever? You are not. You are a terrible judge.

You wonder if your online friends, the people you interact with day and night, look anything like their avatars. You wonder what their offline lives are like.

Better than yours. There's no question about that.

They are probably younger than you, teenagers even. But maybe they're older, really old, retired, infirmed. They could be anywhere in between, like you.

They are not like you. You are not like anyone. If there is one thing you know to be true it's this.

Gambling is also a game.

Life is a game.

Higher stakes.

The highest.

You couldn't pass up free money. All the blinking ads. How could you resist? You were curious. Your friends—your online friends—do it. Terry does it. What could it hurt? It's fun. It's harmless.

You are incapable of learning. Whenever you say

a thing is harmless it nearly destroys you.

So you begin to gamble, a little. And then a little more. You play digital games of chance, poker and roulette. Sometimes you win. You have money in your online account. You earn your own money. They even pay you interest.

You call that earning?

You get a rush from it.

You are a junkie. Your drugs come in many forms. All of them deadly.

It's freedom from being you. You've never been a winner before.

You aren't now.

You used to call it free time.

There is no such animal.

All time is free time when you think about it. It should have been this way from the beginning.

How quickly you forget. You really are dense. Time and life are the same.

179

You gamble with your parents' money, a portion. Maybe one day you'll be able to pay them back. You'll be a big winner.

Who (or is it whom?) are you trying to convince?

Clash of Legends is a never-ending game of strategy and cooperation. It is a universe unto itself. You stockpile weapons and reinforce your army and your compound. You attack and prepare for attack. You defend.

And offend. Or be offended. Don't forget how offensive you are. Now, is that funny? It's all the same to you, isn't it?

You like to throw your new words into the online conversations. You contribute what you can.

You have very little to contribute. After all you are a follower, not a leader.

Bellicosity is a good word. You use it in *Clash of Legends*.

And it is a fitting description of your relationship to the world and to yourself.

Clash of Legends is what gamers call an interactive

collaborative game of military and political strategy.

Call it whatever you want, but it is still a stupid game for idle losers.

When you're playing you don't notice the time. Time doesn't matter. Time flies.

Your silly life flies with it. You don't notice that either.

Terry—if you have to say it, if you are being truthful—is your new best friend. A best friend you've never met in real life. Isn't that weird? You have a lot in common, similar lifestyles. Chris lives a different sort of life.

An imaginary friend, just like when you were young. Well done, you are again a child.

Terry is really into gaming. And gambling. Terry helped get you into gambling.

Pixels of unknown origin on a computer screen told you how to lose your parents' money. Excellent idea. Imaginary Terry sounds like a great friend.

Terry told you which gambling site is the best and why, the one that gives the best odds and bonuses.

Only the best for you, huh? Well, for you and your bestie Terry.

You still spend at least an hour a day—sometimes two—in *Minescraper*. It's fun, but *Clash of Legends* is better, way better, much more challenging, more exciting.

You associate *Clash of Legends* with Terry and that is why you like it. You associate *Minescraper* with Chris and that is why you don't like it. Keep it simple, stupid.

You built an entire village in *Minescraper*. It has everything you'd ever need. You are friends with all the villagers. It is very peaceful, very organized.

But very boring according to Terry, right?

You sometimes worry the games are too much of your life, that they are becoming too real.

You should be worried. You should be terrified. Instead, you indulge in just enough fake worry, just enough false concern, about your pretend life to make you feel better without having to confront the real issue.

At night you sketch strategies and draw

characters on a large notepad: more powerful leaders, less pixilated villagers, various formations, new tactics. You see the games pour from the end of your charcoal pencil. The images come to life.

What is real in your life anyway? What do you have? What can you do? Be honest.

You dream of games, games of strategy and reward. You replay them over and over in your mind. You toss and turn and sometimes sweat. You dream of winning. You dream of sweet victory.

Nothing but sick sticky dreams for you in the shadowed night, unachievable, meaningless dreams.

In the morning, in the pale morning light, you can't wait to get online and play.

This is what is important to you. This is what you've become. It is worse than before.

Your clan is strong. You win battles. Sometimes you lose them. You become a tight knit group. War will do that. It creates deep lasting bonds. It brings you closer together.

It is all illusion. They are illusions. And you are delusional.

You steal from your cleaning time to play more. You shift your schedule.

Your schedule is and always has been a joke, a prop.

Some days you forget to shower. And the laundry piles up.

You are regressing if you know what that means.

Your walks around the block are strolls. You often stop. It is difficult to navigate a real world of sidewalks and stoplights and sudden sounds while staring at your phone.

You are not cut out for the vibrant concrete world of others. You do not have the talents.

Maybe you could get a treadmill and walk at home without obstacles. Play and exercise together.

You were not built for the physical world.

When you lose at poker or roulette you can't wait to play again to win it back. It feels like a little itch that you need to scratch.

Like an infection. And you keep scratching,

184

peeling, pulling, picking at it, like a stupid animal. Necrotizing—wasn't that one of your words?

And why not? You're playing with the house's money.

It is your parents' money. Don't ever forget. Don't you ever.

When you win—and you do—you can't wait to win again.

You lose far more than you win. A fitting metaphor for your life, don't you think?

Chris doesn't come by anymore. You've kind of lost touch. You've gone separate ways. You are always too busy. Chris has work. You have play.

You have to play.

You can play whenever you want.

So you do. So you do.

The routine isn't set in stone. After all, you are the one in charge, aren't you? It's your life.

Is this your life?

Time passes quickly in *Minescraper*. In an hour of play it can go from night to day and back to night. It rains a lot too. Snows.

You think it's just like reality, don't you? You are attempting to seem smart, smarter.

One *Clash of Legends* battle lasted for fourteen hours. And you won. Your clan triumphed. What a thrill! Terry screamed with delight in message after message. It was hard earned but you prevailed. What a battle! Though you were tired you felt alive, you felt like celebrating. For real.

It never rains when Terry is online. You always win with Terry.

So you bought a fifth of vodka. And drank it. And gambled more than you should have. It was not your brightest idea.

Name one bright idea you've ever had. Ever. You, the genius who needed to celebrate an imaginary victory in real life.

You lost a lot of money. You were very unlucky. You had never had such a bad streak before. It was like the games were against you. You kept losing and losing until the vodka and the money were gone. The game wouldn't give you any more credit. You had to shut down.

What a loser.

The gambling site gives you three days before they start charging you interest.

Generous. Hey, maybe they'll send a guy with a thick neck and a baseball bat to your door to collect.

Every Sunday your parents ask you how the job hunt—networking you call it—is going. You tell them that you're plugging away. You say that you are doing your best. You don't tell them about the gambling.

An enormous bearded man to break a kneecap, maybe lop off a finger or two.

Terry offers to help. But the money never arrives.

Another illusion shattered. You can't be sure Terry is a real person. And you gave your address to this Terry character, this stranger. You gave personal information over the Internet.

You tell your parents that it takes time. The world has changed. Every week they send you more money.

You know they can't have that much money. Does it not worry you that they're sacrificing themselves so you can gamble and play?

It isn't the end of the world. Art supplies will have to wait though. Painting put on hold.

Don't you feel guilty? You should.

You have just enough. You can eat like a bird until your parents' next deposit.

Have you ever been this low?

In *Clash of Legends* Terry apologizes. Something came up. An emergency of some sort. It couldn't be helped.

Electronic apologies. Not worth the fake little colored balloons they arrive in.

Your best friend can't help, can't come to your aid. Not like on the battlefield.

Life is not like the battlefield or the battlefield is not like life? You really are an epic idiot.

You stop walking around the block. You go outside less and less. You can't bear to look into peoples' stupid staring quizzical faces.

You are nothing if not consistent.

In the world of online games it's different, more predictable, more supportive. You are always there for one another.

IT IS PRETEND!

There is nothing out of doors for you. Everything you need is within arm's reach. Everything can be found online.

Everything can be simulated online, poorly at that. Nothing online is real.

You eat pizza four or five nights a week. It is fast and easy. You order online. You talk to the delivery boy more than you talk to your parents. You never look him in the eye.

Getting fat should solve your problems. Good plan.

Clash of Legends is a super game. So much fun, exciting. It is uplifting, that's the right word, uplifting, morale boosting.

You can't fake your way out of it this time.

Your parents say you don't look so well. You tell them you are just tired.

You lie—again—to them. You do not deserve such parents. What did they do to deserve you?

In *Clash of Legends* Terry asks you how the gambling is going. You tell Terry you are done with gambling. You are broke.

Breaking. Broken.

Terry suggests trying a different site. A new one. Maybe your luck will change.

There is no such thing as luck. There are only events and actions.

But you don't want to lose any more money. You don't have any money to lose.

You don't have very much of anything.

Terry keeps pestering. All the messages are about gambling.

Yeah, old Terry seems like a real good friend,

good fake people.

You ask Terry why it's so important to gamble.

You dare question the great Terry?

Terry says it's fun, what's the big deal?

The big deal is that you are a loser and always will be. The big deal is that when life is not punching you in the face you hit yourself.

You tell Terry that it's not fun for you. Not anymore. And that's that.

Phonier, more insipid words were never spoken by weaker.

You prepare your troops for the next big battle. Terry has your left flank. You message to review strategy but Terry doesn't answer.

You lost your fake friend. You were too mean.

Terry's green-vested double disappears from the game. Terry disappears.

Aw, you hurt poor imaginary Terry's little imaginary feelings.

You lose the battle. No one in the clan knows why Terry went AWOL. They thought you'd know. They thought you two were close.

What did you really know about your bestie Terry?

You were. Two. Too. Close.

As close as two imaginary avatars can be. Sad.

Terry is nowhere. You search *Minescraper*. You fly over oceans and fields and forests. Searching. But the buildings are empty. The food untouched. Terry is gone.

Good riddance.

Terry will never return.

Terry could return as another character using a different name and you would never know. You never knew Terry. But you thought Terry knew you, didn't you? That's the problem, isn't it?

And you feel sad. You mourn the loss of a friend. You feel empty without Terry. The games do not feel the same. They aren't fun without Terry. You even cry a bit.

What a pathetic creature you are. Go out and make another fake friend if it's so important to you. Or is crying about it more satisfying? Who's going to pity you? Your poor parents? Are you going to beg Chris to return, again? Pathetic.

It occurs to you later, much later, that Terry perhaps played you. That Terry could have been a fraud, a bot paid to get you to gamble. Terry could have pretended to be your friend to steer you to the gambling site. The whole thing could have been a con.

Maybe your friend Terry is out there conning somebody else, laughing at you. Maybe Terry is a Russian mobster or a Nigerian teenager spending Mom and Dad's money on guns and drugs and prostitutes.

By the same token Terry could have been injured, taken ill. Terry could have died. Something, anything, could have happened. There is no way you'll ever know, no way, unless Terry comes back, unless Terry gets in touch, explains.

You want Terry to come back, don't you? Despite the obvious, despite the fact that you were used, you hope that that crook will come back into your life with another blinking message, another encouraging lie.

After all, Terry could have been a ninety-eight-year-old spinster who died of dementia. Terry could have been a twenty-two-year-old student who got run over by a bus. Terry could have been a good person, a great human being. Terry could have been anybody.

Terry could have been anybody but you. Terry was not a loser.

Without Terry and Chris *Minescraper* is no fun. You abandon your village. It is soon swallowed by the electronic jungle. And your once powerful clan in *Clash of Legends* disbands after another ugly loss. You quit battling. Never again will you get to be Gilgamesh or Joan of Arc. Never again will you be part of a tight-knit clan. Terry is gone. Game-playing is over.

Is it time to grow up now?

A STORY OF STORYTELLERS

Writers play games. It comes with the territory. It is part of the process. Sometimes it keeps us sane. As writers we play with words. We play with characters. We play with lives, real and fictitious. We play with time and we play with place. Play is an inescapable side effect of prolonged isolation and introspection. It is the vampish price of imagination. Writers are constantly playing. I am writing this, but I am playing too. I am playing with word order and cadence. I am playing with the truth and I am playing with the reader. I am playing with *you*. And if you've come this far you must be enjoying the game. I confess that I am too. These essays, all these stories, are products of the mind—both mine and yours. That is how storytelling works. This entire book, whatever it may be, is a figment of our minds. We are creating it together, becoming one mind. And the mind plays tricks.

Once upon a time in the early 1980s a well-known, highly acclaimed British author played a little trick on the publishing world, a public game. She pretended to be someone else. She pretended to be unknown. She played a joke on those who knew her writing best.

To demonstrate the struggle unknown writers face and to prove that *nothing succeeds like success*, this successful and respected author—she would go on to win a Nobel Prize—submitted two new novels to her publisher under a pseudonym. Her game was a test of sorts. Her longtime publisher, who shall remain nameless, turned the books down flat. She received a form letter rejection. He claimed the novels wouldn't sell. He failed her test. Eventually both books were accepted by another British publisher and by Knopf in the United States.

Acceptance and publication, however, were only part of the story. Their reception, or should I say lack thereof, was the second act. Though the books were generally well-reviewed, neither made much of an impact in the literary world. The novels were ignored. Sales were weak. The first—*Diary of a Good Neighbor*—sold three thousand copies, whereas the second—*If the Old Could . . . .*—sold but fifteen hundred. This was an inauspicious debut at best.

Our famous author—for the purposes of her scheme rebranding herself Jane Somers—also sent the books to several reviewers, those who had reviewed her books in the past. It was another test, another game, another target. Not one of them recognized the prose, not a single one recognized the true author.

After a short time the well-known author revealed her deception. She had proved her point. She was satisfied. The two novels were rereleased under her real name and sales predictably soared. Indeed nothing succeeds like success. The longtime publisher was satisfied too. He was correct in his judgment that the Jane Somers books wouldn't sell very well. Fame helps sales. Every simpleton knows that. They all had a good laugh. It was a harmless prank. But did the stunt prove anything? Did our author or anyone else involved learn from the deception?

Some contend that the Jane Somers experiment was simply a devious way for the author to humiliate the reviewing community. Each one of the hand-picked reviewers had recently panned her latest books—a short series of science fiction novels—an ill-advised departure from what had made her famous, according to most critics. Were her public-spirited motives mere pretense? Was her game one of revenge? Was it personal?

The Jane Somers hoax was long forgotten by 2007 when renowned novelist and feminist Doris Lessing received the Nobel Prize for Literature. Not many cared to recall when Lessing played at being Somers.

Lessing died in 2013. Her little game warranted a passing mention, no more. I cannot ask her to relive the experience and comment on her motivations. I cannot ask her if she learned anything from the trick. Her literary stunt will remain but a footnote in publishing history. Her intentions are no longer debated. It must remain enough that she once sought pseudonymity. As good writers are wont to do she fiddled with her characters, with her readers, and with our expectations.

Not long after William Jefferson Clinton won the United States presidential election of 1992 a roman à clef entitled *Primary Colors* depicting life on the campaign trail was released. The book spent nine weeks atop the *New York Times* bestseller list. The author of the thinly veiled portrait was Anonymous.

The novel is neither good nor bad. It isn't particularly witty or insightful. It breaks no new ground. The appeal is its peek behind closed doors. It is purely *fly-on-the-wall* prurience, political voyeurism. The plotline is trite. Idealistic Henry Burton joins the campaign staff of charismatic Jack Stanton and becomes increasingly disillusioned. That's the story.

From the very beginning the book's anonymous authorship was seen as a marketing gimmick. It was seen as a tool. It was a way to inject mystery and gossip into the sordid airing of dirty laundry. It was a trick to move more books. It was hype. It was a game. Most critics treated it as such despite one reviewer's claim that *anonymity makes truthfulness much easier.*

Even before its anticipated release, reviewers and insiders had a pretty good idea who held the pen behind Anonymous. There were only so many people with the necessary campaign access, only so many people who could have been that thousand-eyed fly on the wall. The author's prose provided additional clues. Computers did the rest. After analyzing the data a linguistics professor from Vassar was convinced he'd identified the writer with almost one hundred percent certitude. He made his bold claim on national television. He outed the author. The professor was angrily denounced by the accused who staked his journalistic reputation on his denials. The game continued a bit longer.

Six months of deception ended in true confession. The belittled professor from Vassar had been correct. The author's journalistic reputation apparently meant nothing. No one was very surprised. No one very much cared. The author wasn't famous enough. He wasn't interesting. The charade had been meaningless. It had been a stunt. It had sold books. A movie starring John Travolta was made. Like the book it wasn't very good either. Another thing to be forgotten. The public quickly turned the page. The author might as well have remained anonymous.

Was it all about marketing or was Anonymous something of a coward? Was he perhaps concerned his overt criticism of the newly elected popular president was career suicide? Was he worried he had betrayed real people who had put their trust in him, real people who would be hurt by his unflattering portrayals? Was he afraid he'd played too fast and loose with people's lives? I have no idea. You'll have to ask him yourself, if you can find him. He'd probably love the opportunity to talk about it.

The author of *Primary Colors* is still among us so I won't comment further. He can explain his motivations better than I ever could. He was there, wasn't he? Why put your trust in a biased secondary source? Let him defend the decision. Let him blame it on the publisher. Let him hide behind his not-so-veiled characters. I'll leave it to him. He is now known to all, although, he too, has largely been forgotten. After all, he was Anonymous for less than a year.

The uber-rich are never satisfied and the richest author in the world wanted more. There is always more to be had, always another challenge. Diffidence doesn't get you rich. She wanted more. (In her defense, how many billionaires are content with what they already have?)

I don't have to tell you who she is. I won't spell out her name. You know her. You have seen her face on the covers of magazines and book jackets. You know her bespectacled wizard and his magical school. You've seen the movies and visited the attraction parks. You may have even plunked down ten pounds to have your photo taken in a London train station beside a stuffed white owl. Maybe. Maybe not. Either way I'm sure she has some of your money. I know she has some of mine.

In 2013 the Little Brown company published *The Cuckoo's Calling*, the debut novel of Robert Galbraith — a former plainclothes Royal Military Police investigator. The detective novel, depending on your source, sold between five hundred and fifteen hundred copies. Despite being called a *stellar debut* and reviewed positively by the press, sales were anemic. This would soon change.

Speculation started that Robert Galbraith was an imposter, that no such RMP man ever existed. The questioning began before the book was released. There were clues strewn everywhere. Galbraith, the book's presumed author, shared the same agent and editor as the richest, most famous author in the world. This was odd luck for a fledgling crime writer. More questions were asked. The arts editor for the *Sunday Times* decided to dig deeper. *The Cuckoo's Calling* was submitted for linguistic analysis. There were just too many coincidences. Eventually the editor called the big bluff and confronted the agent who immediately—and no doubt happily—confessed. The creator of the boy wizard with the lightning bolt scar on his forehead and Robert Galbraith were one in the same person. The literary ruse had lasted all of six weeks.

Following the agent's admission, Little Brown rushed an additional one hundred and forty thousand copies to print. They were quickly sold. No one was surprised. Little Brown was in on the Galbraith game from the get go. It was not much of a gamble for a publisher who knew all along the truth would surface. It was only a question of when. They may have even been the ones who started the speculation. The book is still in print. It still sells well. The richest author in the world has written three more detective novels under the name Robert Galbraith. They have sold equally well. She gets richer and richer. Everyone knows who is behind Robert Galbraith, but they pretend not to know. One more little game readers and writers play.

Was this case of transgender pseudonymity a

cynical marketing ploy? Was it just another *Primary Colors*-type gimmick? It depends on who you ask. It certainly garnered publicity for the *debut* work. Everyone involved made money. But surely the billionaire wasn't after greater riches. There has to be another explanation. Perhaps it was an artist's honest attempt to break free from expectations à la Lessing with her science fiction. Perhaps the richest writer in the world writes detective novels better under a man's name. Perhaps this is her creative way of playing the macho detective.

Like the author of *Primary Colors*, the writer of wizards and detectives is alive and well able to tell her own story. My speculations are pointless. If you are curious you'll find her. Ask her sometime. She's on Twitter. She tweets a lot. Maybe she'll tell you.

Writers play. It comes with the territory. They play with their books and, sometimes, they play with their own lives, always adding and subtracting. Games can be difficult to stop once you get used to them. Lines blur. A writer always plays many roles. Anonymity and pseudonymity are easy ways to play at real life. And sometimes it sells more books too.

REHAB

You study the obvious. You will never learn.

You will always be learning, life is learning.

Not until you are in a box and covered in dirt: dead and buried.

There is so much to know and so much to share.

It is all pretend, this life of yours, a pretty façade. Just like the stupid games you used to play.

If you could get down to what's real and true then you'd have a chance. Knowledge, learning, can get you there. It's a path.

You want to know something? You killed your parents. That's what's real. That's what's true. That's knowledge.

Reading helps. Sharing the pain helps. *On Death & Dying.*

Reading about grief won't save you. Online weeping won't help you. You are beyond that. Your situation is different. After all, they are dead because of you.

The hurt will never go away completely. That's what they all say, the experts. You learned that much.

You should read about homicide instead. *How I Killed My Parents Without Really Trying*. You should share your crimes. Share that knowledge.

They left you when you needed them most, when you were most vulnerable. They were old. It was their time. They didn't mean to.

How does a murderer grieve? When does a sociopath say sorry? They pretend to mourn.

They were your only family, your best friends, the only ones who loved you.

Your selfishness has no limit. It exceeds all. It stains everything.

You will be better. You can be better.

You think you can change? Atone?

They won't be here to see it, but you will change. If not for yourself, for them.

Have you ever?

You are a human being. You are capable of change. You have worth.

You think you have value? LOL. You are a degenerate waste of space and resources.

You can help others.

You are the definition of moronic.

You can inspire and encourage others to be better, to be the best they can be.

You engage in online masturbation with other morons. And you call that change. What good can come of it?

You post on politics and painting. You want the world to be better, to be more beautiful. You can help. You can lead.

Your comments and your thoughts are childish and uninformed. Your arguments are empty and pointless. You can't step outside your apartment but you think you can lead others. And follow you where?

The national election is important. It is meaningful. Some say it is the most important election ever, a turning point, a crossroads.

Nothing is important. You'll never learn, will you?

Compassionate politics and creative arts are worth fighting for. They are important.

And what about your drinking? Surely drinking is important. Don't forget drinking. Don't forget the sweet sting of cold vodka. Don't you remember how it helps you forget?

Drinking helps you mourn. It gets you through long, dark, lonely nights and troubling days. It helps.

It helps.

You have always been sensitive, like an artist. Inside you have always thought like an artist. It is time to become one.

You can't just decide to become an artist.

Artists feel. They observe. They know. Their knowledge goes beyond language, beyond intelligence.

You don't know how to paint. You can't draw. You don't know what it means to be an artist.

You feel you are an artist. You feel artistic. It is in

your nature.

You are making a fool of yourself. Others read your inane comments and laugh. They are amused and encouraged by your oblivious stupidity.

You share your sentiments with others. You share your hopes and your dreams and your work.

Your so-called *art*: tasteless scribbles, colored scratches on canvas, praised only by your now dead parents.

You discuss your work. You comment on the work of others. Some of it is good, some of is not so good. But you try to be encouraging, you try to help.

Compliments paid for with worry and premature death.

You are not seeking praise. You want to help make a change. You want to make a difference.

But you aren't. You only succeed in hurting your cause. You are destroying what you pretend to care about.

You are different. You are an artist. Political artists have the power to change the world.

You can't change who you are.

You tell others they can be whatever they want to be.

The others are laughing.

You can change. You have changed. Life and death have changed you.

You have difficulties changing your socks.

You are a mentor.

You'll never be the person you want to be. It is an ideal. It is an impossibility.

You are a teacher.

You are a killer.

You are alone. No one can help. You must go it alone, heroically.

Confess, murderer.

You can help others by sharing your pain, sharing your struggles and sharing your work.

Words won't help you. Pictures won't make it better.

Equivoque is a charming word. It is today's word. You like it.

You only like the word because it has two qs. You've already forgotten what it means. You really are a colossal idiot.

You don't like every word. Some you already know. But you will keep learning. You will keep trying to learn.

Studying great artists only teaches that you will never be anything like them. It is a study in your own inability, a study in your unique and futile ineptitude. It is a study in failure.

You miss your mom and dad.

You didn't even go to the funeral. Funerals.

They gave you everything. Whatever you do, whatever you become, belongs to them.

They gave you life. Little did they know.

And now you can give back to others. You can

help. This is your mission.

The art students—the objects of your grand mission—make fun of you. You are too old to become an artist. You are too stupid. And you have no talent. They are young and hopeful and skilled. You have nothing in common. You have nothing to teach.

You have experience. You have your art.

They indulge you. It makes them feel better about their own prospects. You are a warning, a joke. They mock you. They pity you.

You try to be constructive in your comments, encouraging.

You pretend you know more than you know. You pretend you know more than they do. You take puny jabs at their hope with misplaced words.

You try to help. Sometimes the truth hurts.

You pick at their technique and poke at their dreams. You are a coward.

A poltroon is a coward.

You are a poltroon then.

You know the truth has hurt you. Too many times.

You hide behind lame pseudonyms, schools of thought, the words of others.

You tell them what would work better, how to improve.

You are the lowest of the low.

It is all for the greater good, you tell yourself.

You should be ashamed. You should be arrested.

You thought you would be detained, at least questioned.

Another stupid nightmare dashed by daybreak.

It is not your fault.

Even if you didn't pull the trigger, you still killed them. If you're not being hunted it is due to apathy or chance.

You have to go on. Helping others helps you. It gives you purpose.

You will always be a fugitive.

You learned a lot once upon a time. You studied. There are techniques you learned that they no longer teach.

You don't even hold the brush the way they do. You don't have the eye.

You share what you know. It helps.

You can't hold a brush to them. Your strokes are timid and unsure.

Reclamation is the word.

Another new word? How will you use it?

The world has become a scary place. The choice is clear. Either press forward and make the world better or return to the darkness. The choice is ours. The time is now.

Never has a comment so inane been so poorly written. You will never raise an army that way.

The vote is our weapon.

They'll all laugh about that one. You really

outdid yourself. You really displayed the depth of your naïve ignorance.

Art suffers when people suffer. Art is the prize of an enlightened people. But it must be fought for. No one can appreciate art when they are worrying about putting food on the table or a roof over their head. Art can help people, but only when people are taken care of.

Politics is about people, their wants and needs. It is about governing. You know nothing about what people want. You know nothing about real people. You never have. You don't even know what *you* want, do you? You couldn't govern yourself.

People want to be happy. You want to be happy.

You really are an idiot. You are the Mariana Trench of ignorance. Do you know where that is? Do you know what a trench is?

Everyone is entitled to their opinion, but a fact is a fact.

And your opinion is wrong. You are wrong. Time and time again. Wrong. Wrong. Wrong.

There is a tsunami of disinformation, fake news

and rumors, a flood of hate.

You are all wet.

If everything looks like an enemy one will always live in hateful fear.

You think you're clever, an expert, you think your words possess weight? Why, because you read a few articles, because you know a few names, a few cherry-picked facts, because you have formed an opinion?

Facts are facts and cannot be changed.

Even your facts are suspect.

Your beliefs are challenged. Your facts are called into question. The opposition is relentless. But you will not give up. Not this time. You are a hero.

There are too many of them. They are the real experts. They know too much. They will shout you down if they have to. They will crush you. You can't win. You will never change them. It is another impossibility.

You can't change them. You can't change what they believe. But you can do what you think is right.

You can try. History is full of people who never tried.

You are trying. You don't know history. You don't know shit. But you *are* trying.

You know that this is important.

Tilting at windmills. Have you ever heard the expression?

Your fight for humanity is a battle for the importance of art itself.

You are afraid to leave your apartment. You don't know how to hold a brush.

You work, you comment, you paint.

Or make a point.

You won't give in.

You can't mix colors. You can't create.

Art is the measure of our humanity. Art is civilization's prize. Art makes living worthwhile.

You can't manage a decent cup of coffee or a cogent argument.

215

You can change things.

You are gray. Your life is gray. It is all dark gray.

You have changed.

Your arguments are foggy and dense.

You share what you feel. You write about what matters. You hope.

You are angering people. You are making enemies. And these are real people, posting under their real names. They are political professionals. Actual people who know what they're talking about. And they are mad at you.

No work of art, no worthy opinion, is met with unqualified praise.

For what you said. For what you wrote, so clumsily, so unthinkingly.

You are honest. You do not hold back. The truth hurts.

In some countries people are executed for their words.

Your parents are dead. You have no one to protect, nothing to lose.

People are hunted and killed for saying the wrong thing.

You share what you believe is right. You are doing what is right.

Politics is for keeps, it is life and death, not like your meaningless art.

There are always consequences to acting. There are consequences to not acting too.

And yet you keep writing, you continue to comment, to post.

You try not to hurt anyone. You try not to respond to personal attacks.

Parents are slain too.

You try to reason with them.

You think you are creating change with your stupid comments.

You try to see their side and you try to get them

217

to understand yours.

No one gives a damn what you have to say. About anything.

Blandishment was yesterday's word.

It's just another useless word.

Sometimes you think your words are useless. Your paintings speak much louder.

You think your artwork will get you noticed, respected? You think showing your dusty pieces will make a difference? You think posting your theories will win you friends and admirers? You think you'll become famous, don't you? That's what's behind all this change talk.

You are helping.

Your art comments are as bad as your political opinions.

You have experience to share.

No, in fact they are worse. Art assaults the eyes as well as the mind.

You try to be constructive.

You believe you are an agent of change, a rebel political artist. You are out to save the world. And through bad art no less.

The world changes all the time. Who says it cannot change for the better? Who says an artist cannot lead the way? Who says an artist cannot be a hero?

It is laughable. You aren't even meant for the world you are working to save. You don't fit in. You aren't cut out for it. You do not have the ability. You do not have the talent.

You are an artist.

And you killed your parents.

You are a painter.

And you can't draw.

You are a caring human being.

And you are being ridiculed. You are so pathetic you can't even spot the sarcasm.

You are helping.

Your good friend Terry is probably one of your mockers. You'd never know.

You try to ignore the rude comments from automated accounts or those itching for a fight.

If you really thought you were right, if you really thought you had talent, if you really believed in your cause, you wouldn't give a damn what anybody said.

You respectfully and thoughtfully share your opinions.

According to current law you do have a right to your opinion, even if it's wrong.

You try not to argue.

And it's always wrong.

You believe you are right.

When have you been right?

You believe you are an artist.

But you *know* you are a murderer.

You believe it is important.

You deserve their scorn. You deserve to be buried by their foul words. And you deserve much worse.

You are a human being.

The word is parricide.

You are one of many.

You won't vote.

Trying to make the world a better place.

You can't paint.

You are one who paints.

Go ahead, have another drink. It's tasty, icy and refreshing. You'll make better art. It'll make your comments sharper. It will loosen your thoughts and free your hand. The genius will flow like vodka.

Art is often beyond understanding.

What can it hurt?

Politics can be complex.

Who cares?

You try to help.

And they all make fun of you. That's how they get their fun.

It isn't fun. It feels like work. It is hard. It is worthwhile.

Don't you recognize them? Don't you see that they have same names, the same handles?

You feel you are fighting an uphill battle.

They are called trolls.

You try to see their side.

You are a troll too, a cave troll.

You are an artist.

You are clueless.

You believe some ideas are better than other ideas. You will not apologize for that. Truth is always the best path.

You comment on their comments. You post. And you quarrel. You tell them they are wrong, confused. You attack their beliefs. That makes you a troll.

You are working for the greater good.

Dialectic is the word. What do you know?

You know that you are doing your best.

You've been called worse. But you'll be lucky if it stops at name-calling.

You can win. You are more determined than you've ever been.

You'll never win.

You believe you are right.

You are worse.

You are better than that.

Of course you have a reply for that too.

You are trying to help. You are trying to make the world better.

Don't send another. This is not your fight.

You have to keep trying. You have to keep posting. You have to keep painting.

You'll only make it worse.

Or what is the point?

Do not hit send.

Send.

Delete it.

Sent.

A WORLD ONLINE

And overnight the entire world changed and we were under attack from phishermen, trolls, and cyber-bullies. Overnight everything was interconnected. Overnight everyone had a voice. And it was virtual babel, a proliferation of promiscuity. The balance of power had shifted. Everyone was someone else. Handles and avatars threatened with a wink and a smile. The world online became a dangerous space. A world that once held so much pleasure and promise had devolved into a digital cesspool, a non-stop pseudonymous playground for the depraved.

It wasn't supposed to be like this, of course. Internet users were never meant to be anonymous. The online world was built to work like the mail system with verifiable addresses and trusted, accountable providers. It wasn't intended to be a hideout. It wasn't designed to enable evil. User names were for identification, not for cruelty, not to protect criminal conduct. The Internet was supposed to be open and civilized and efficient and beautiful, egalitarian. But the world had other ideas. The world changed. And, like it or not, the Internet led this change.

And so we drown in a bottomless ocean of anonymous information.

Wikipedia and WikiLeaks may share the same first four letters but they are not the same. They are different entities with different goals and different missions. And yet they share one gigantic problem.

Wikipedia, started in 2001 by Jimmy Wales, is the world's foremost free online encyclopedia. WikiLeaks, formed in 2006 by Julian Assange, is a not-for-profit publisher of secret information, news leaks and classified material from anonymous sources. Both enterprises traffic in factual electronically published information. This is where the similarities end and the problems begin.

Wikipedia consistently ranks among the top ten sites visited on the Internet. It is gargantuan and influential and grows larger and more important every single day. As of 2012, more than five million articles were available on the English language version of Wikipedia. Over three hundred thousand editors edit Wikipedia every month. More than eight hundred thousand editors have edited articles more than twenty times. It is an unrelenting, massive undertaking, which would not be possible without the hundreds of thousands of anonymous, unheralded, and unpaid writers, editors, and researchers. Wikipedia is the people's information, it is by the people, it is for the people. It is an open forum. Anyone can write or rewrite an article. Anyone can edit the encyclopedia.

And that's the issue, isn't it? That's the root of the problem. Machines may be able to manage and post all that information. People—human beings—are losing ground. No one can guarantee the constant accuracy of so much information, of so many details. No manmade force can police every alteration. It is too much. It is too encyclopedic. As a result Wikipedia suffers from mistakes and inaccuracies. The site is continually plagued by downright lies and misinformation. Sure, dedicated editors try to keep up. They try to clean up the mess. They do their best to amend and to correct and to get it right. But when I visit a Wikipedia article—when I research—I have no way of verifying the accuracy of the information. I don't know whether I'm reading fact or fiction. If I am interested in the factual truth I have to go to secondary sources to see if they concur. And that's wrong. What kind of encyclopedia needs secondary verification? The process is backwards. It's reversed the arrow of truth. It's a pain. It's laborious. So we don't do it. We don't verify. We simply accept that Wikipedia, for all its flaws, is our gospel, our shared truth, the people's truth. And in doing so we further disseminate falsehoods and untruths. Worse, we lose the ability to believe . . . in anything. In this encyclopedic sea of information we are losing our bearings. We do not know what is real or what is true anymore and we are sinking. Is there anything more frightening?

WikiLeaks positions itself as a kind of digital *Pentagon Papers*. Despite having no headquarters, sustained by public donations, and dependent on anonymous whistle-blowers for content, WikiLeaks has irked and irritated governments and corporations around the globe by publishing and publicizing countless illegalities, transgressions and moral failings. From his sanctum in an Ecuadorean embassy, Aussie Julian Assange unabashedly threatens to destabilize the world's geopolitical structure by airing its darkest secrets. Nothing is off limits. Nothing is sacrosanct. And therein lies the flaw. Ultimately, the WikiLeaks model relies on anonymous sources with debatable reasons for disseminating secret, proprietary, classified and, often, unverifiable information. Yes, WikiLeaks does its best to vet the information. But they cannot fact-check every detail. They cannot guarantee light amid so much darkness. And they certainly cannot contextualize the information. It is too much. Again we are swamped with questionable data and conjecture. So, unless the information touches me personally, unless it is about the government spying on *me* or hacking *my* electronic vote for president, I, like many others, ignore WikiLeaks for the most part. I ignore the geopolitical complexities swirling around me. It's all too much, too nebulous. Life is hard enough. I have other problems. I have other things to worry about. So do you.

And we put our trust in anonymous currency.

Money is a sham. At best you can say that money is a proxy. Printed or minted it is another game we all agree to play. We accept that a particular right-angled parallelogram of colored paper has a determined value. Theoretically its worth, its agreed-upon value, is backed by a recognized nation, a sovereign power, some agreed-upon authority. This is not the case in the new world of digital pelf.

Bitcoin is a crypto-currency and digital payment system invented by an unknown programmer using a phony Japanese-sounding name. Its monetary policy is based on artificial scarcity. There will always be a limited supply of bitcoins. (New bitcoins are *mined* at a continually adjusted rate and the world—the Internet world—will, if current projections are accurate, excavate the last bitcoin around 2040.) Released into the online world in 2009 by the fictitious Satoshi Nakamoto, bitcoin is a peer-to-peer system, no intermediaries needed, no banks required. Bitcoin is pseudonymous. Funds are not tied to real-world entities but rather bitcoin addresses. It is the ninja of currencies.

By 2015 there were over one hundred thousand legitimate merchants and vendors who accepted bitcoins. Bitcoin is gaining legitimacy. More and more real people are signing up to play the bitcoin game. By 2020 it is estimated that more than ten million merchants will have joined the fun. And there is no telling how many illegitimate transactions involve this anonymous payment system. It is a coin designed for criminal activity. Law enforcement estimates vary so widely they are useless. We do know that since its inception bitcoin has been the preferred method of payment for online drug and arms dealers, fences and thieves, pimps, pedophiles, and hackers. Bitcoin's intrinsic anonymity is a criminal's dream.

But what if the mysterious Satoshi Nakamoto figuratively reappears and decides to release more bitcoins into the ether? Or fewer? There have already been several highly publicized bitcoin robberies. And entire bitcoin warehouses have gone bankrupt. The value of the bitcoin has fluctuated insanely from five dollars to more than fifteen thousand. There is still no international consensus on crypto-currency. Instability will continue. Is bitcoin a scam? Is it a Ponzi scheme destined to one day crumble under the weight of its coding? Or is this crypto-currency the beginning of a world that no longer requires physical, tangible methods of payment? Could this be the dawning of something even bigger? Another petty nuisance eradicated through the binary magic of information technology. Will everything—even us, even human beings, the creators—one day exist only online, only in code? Will all become simulacrum? Thankfully, I won't be around to find out. Maybe you will. Maybe your children will. In the meantime I do know that unless we agree that something has value, it doesn't. Money requires consensus. Bitcoin may never get there. Then again, maybe it has already surpassed us all.

And where in the world would we be without eponymous Anonymous.

Anonymous portray themselves as the Merry Pranksters of the Internet. In their pursuit of lulz—web jargon for schadenfreude, shits and grins at another's expense—these hacktivists patrol the online universe righting perceived wrongs, speaking binary truth to power. Anonymous is a shadowy Robin Hood organization, a nebulous international network of militant entities, which, depending on your viewpoint, is populated by freedom fighters or cyber terrorists, programmer white hats or online lynch mobs. They call themselves an *internet gathering . . . that operates on ideas rather than directives*. And, according to their ideas, their existence is needed to protect us from ourselves.

Through distributed denial-of-service (DDoS) attacks and other hacking stratagems, members of Anonymous (anons) disrupt government, religious and corporate websites. There is no single agenda. Broadly speaking anons oppose Internet censorship and control. Members have hacked the Church of Scientology and PayPal. They have targeted the U.S. Copyright Office and Sony. They have supported the Arab Spring and Occupy Wall Street. They are everywhere and they are nowhere. In 2012 *Time* called Anonymous one of the *one hundred most influential people in the world*.

Any computer, anywhere, can be a target of Anonymous, and for any reason. They are cyber vigilantes beholden to no one. Anons pay no dues, sign no contract, carry no membership card. All you have to do to be a member of Anonymous is declare yourself a member. And, unsurprisingly, not all members are in it for the lulz. There are anons who are anarchists and

231

anons who are trolls. Some anons are common criminals, Internet thieves, and cyber con artists. Malevolent programmers sometimes hide their identities and destructive malware behind the Guy Fawkes mask of Anonymous. Most of us have nothing to fear from the anons. We are small fish. They are not interested in us. But, as human beings, we tend to fear what we do not understand. And we do not understand the Internet. We do not recognize this new online world. We do not know how it operates. But we do know that even the best intentions can go sideways. Anonymous is scary because they possess a novel and special power, a behind-the-scenes, algorithm-encoded power that cannot be seen, only felt. Anonymous has the power to reach into our digitized dreams and short-circuit our real-time lives. Such power is terrifying. Such a world is flimsy. Anonymous alone does not make being online more threatening. But are we any safer when they logon?

The world knows the names of Jimmy Wales and Julian Assange. They have made themselves famous. They have chosen to become personalities. The world does not know the anonymous worker bees and informants behind the famous names. A few Anonymous members have been caught and arrested, but the group is like an iceberg, largely hidden. I suppose it is only fitting that the true power—the real engineers behind the cold, unfeeling system of information that is the Internet—remains anonymous.

It makes sense in an increasingly isolated yet hyper-interconnected world. The Internet should remain faceless, the curtain drawn. Even if I could I wouldn't dox the people pulling the binary strings behind the screen. Anonymity is what we have come to expect. It is what we deserve.

The Internet was supposed to be a reflection of an open and civilized society, a mirror of our dreams and aspirations. And, sadly, maybe that is what it's become. Maybe as a species we are that depraved and cruel, unable or unwilling to escape our bestial nature. Maybe we enjoy harming more than helping. Maybe evil is louder and stronger than good. Maybe for a time we just foolishly convinced ourselves otherwise. Maybe we presumed technology would improve us, make us better. Instead the online world became a hood for the hoods. And the dark net—the deep web—became a lair. We are all hiding behind pseudonyms now. We don't recognize ourselves anymore. I don't recognize myself. When I look into the Internet all I see is fear. What do you see?

RECON

Delete your accounts.

Why would you do that? Even if you could.

Every. Single. One.

You can't. You won't. You can't imagine doing so.

You are no longer welcome anywhere online. It is unfortunate.

You are part of the community. You are liked and respected. You have earned the right to interact.

All of them.

You will not do it.

You are not worthy.

You are valued.

Get offline.

The idea is absurd.

You are the enemy.

You are the savior.

Do it.

You stopped drinking. No more vodka.

You need your liquid courage now more than ever.

You won't disconnect.

You will be taught a lesson.

You are the instructor. You learn and you teach.

Delete your accounts.

You will not.

Now!

No!

You are the enemy.

You are the liberator.

Power down. Unplug the laptop. Turn off the lights. Hide in the cracked walls like the rat you are.

You will not hide. You will not cower. You will stand tall, metaphorically, that is, online.

You are pathetic.

You are a champion.

You are exposed.

You are free.

You were warned.

You were harassed.

You fought and lost.

You fight and continue to fight.

You are hunted.

You are helping.

You interfered. You boasted. You are a bully. You are a troll.

You argued. You battled. You are a hero. You are the light.

You chose the wrong horse, the dark horse. You mocked.

You fight for what is right. You battle for what is important.

For the sake of your ego you made enemies.

You fight for others, not yourself.

You are small. You are mean.

You are small, but you are not alone. You are committed. You are not the only one.

The election is over.

The election is over.

Your team lost. You lost. You've lost everything.

You lost a battle. You did not lose the war. The war can't be lost. Humanity ends if you lose the war.

Nothing ever ends.

You fought. You are still fighting. There are many paths to victory.

You've never mattered.

You matter. Ideas and art matter.

It is a matter of public record.

You did your best. You do your best.

You never mattered.

The war is not about you. It is about decency. It is about righteousness.

Where are your pretty words now?

You believe in what is right.

Your words are public record. Everything about you is public. And publicity leads to destruction and death.

You are more than a file. You are more than words and numbers on a page, more than black on white, more than scratches. You are a human being. You are an artist.

Your artists have logged off, gone underground with their easels and their tubes of paint. They cannot help. They have fled.

All artists work alone.

You artsy *friends* have left you. You've been abandoned.

Everyone leaves eventually.

Political art is the enemy. Art is the new enemy. You are the enemy.

You are the only hope.

Art lost. Your ideas lost. Your side lost. You lost.

You have just begun to fight.

You are alone. Does it feel familiar? It hurts, doesn't it?

Every day is a brand new day. Every dawn reverses night's darkness. Every day brings new hope.

So you continue to post. You continue to search. You keep trying.

You will never stop trying.

You were warned and yet you persist.

You were called names. You were abused and badmouthed. It didn't stop you.

You will pay.

You will win. In the end. You will not stop.

This time it's no empty threat. You are wanted. You are in danger. You are the prey, a lamb to be slaughtered.

You are the redeemer. You are one of many. You will die for the cause. You are not afraid to die.

You made no difference. You created no artists, launched no movement. You lost the vote. You didn't help. You weren't a hero.

You made a difference. You helped many souls. You helped. You guided. You fought the good fight.

And you won't stop. Even after losing.

All is not lost.

Now you're going to pay the price.

You are not afraid.

Enemies must be buried.

Opponents should be shown the errors of their ways.

Sooner or later you will pay.

Everyone pays in the end.

Getting offline won't help you now. It is too late.

You can't stop.

You have lost.

You don't lose until you stop trying.

The art students lost too. But they were clever enough to sense defeat. They hid. They escaped. They too will be captured.

You live to fight another day.

They were never on your side. They never listened. They were never committed to your cause.

241

You are one among many. You are connected.

They laughed at you. They made fun of you.

You are part of a social movement, an online revolution.

They never needed you. They never wanted you. They never asked for you.

You are valued.

They are gone. Too.

You do what you have to do when you have to do it. You do. All do.

They are smart, smarter than you. They all are.

You are a leader and an inspiration.

You are a laughingstock and a loser. And soon you'll be dead.

You will continue the fight.

You are in real trouble.

You know the score. The game is not over.

You have no one.

You have been alone most of your life. It is your lot.

You can't go out. You can't log off. You wouldn't survive.

You will survive. That is what you do.

What to do?

You will find a way.

Your murdered parents can't come to your rescue.

You didn't ask for help. You only asked to be heard, to be listened to.

And you honestly believed that hiding behind pseudonyms would protect you?

You never hid, not intentionally.

You thought user names and fake facts would protect your anonymity. Well, aren't you just the perfect little idiot?

Anonymity is a blunt tool. Your anonymity came naturally. It always does.

You were always a nobody, a fraud. You never understood anything.

You understand the importance of the battle. You understand the stakes.

It was all play for you, wasn't it? You pretended to be a hero. You pretended to be an artist.

You are a hero. You are an artist. No one can take that away from you.

Now you will pay.

You will never give up.

You figured you were safe? You thought you were anonymous? Really?

You fought with the only weapons you had. And that will not stop.

You keep at it. You keep pushing. You will never learn.

You have to stand up for your beliefs. You have

to fight for your principles.

And for what? To what end?

Or what is it for? Where is the meaning?

User names and handles and excuses and words and art are meaningless.

Meaning is personal. Death is impersonal.

Winning and action and success define the good life.

Definitions change. The meaning of a word can change.

You will be hunted. You will be captured and killed.

You will die someday, no matter what.

Terry could be after you. Or a bearded man.

Few face death's angel twice.

Terry could be anyone. Terry could wear a beard. You wouldn't know.

You have no real friends. You have no one to protect. So you protect all. You fight for all.

Terry trolled you. You trolled Terry.

You will fight until the end.

The world is nothing but trolls and liars. You are a part of the world. Ergo. You never grasped that bit of logic, did you?

The world can be so much better than it is. It doesn't have to be this way.

Some trolls are born winners. Some trolls are born losers. You are a loser, born and bred.

It's shameful. The world is wonderful.

Anyone could be after you. All it takes is one.

All it takes is one determined person to start a movement.

You played the game. You enjoyed it. It made you feel special.

You can't change the world if you don't try.

You gambled.

You can't make the world a better place without effort.

It was rigged.

There is always hope. You will always have hope.

You angered the wrong people.

Change—any kind of change—is painful.

And you lost. Big time.

And great change, whether individual or societal, requires great pain, great sacrifice.

You will pay the consequences. Losers always do.

Victory never endures. Tomorrow's battle erases today's memory.

You will be destroyed.

You are trying to save the world, not see it destroyed.

Getting offline will not be enough. It is too late for that. It will not save you.

You do not care about your welfare. You are beyond that.

You will be tracked down and killed. Like a rat.

You are a savior.

You are a traitor.

You are a patriot.

You are a traitor to humanity.

You are humanity's hope.

You are a living, breathing disappointment to your sacrificed parents.

You are no longer a disappointment to yourself.

You lost.

You will win.

The instant you went online you became part of the problem, that's when life ended for you. The moment you chose a mouse over men you were doomed.

With a mouse, with a little laptop, you chose to risk it all to help mankind knowing that it could cost you. You made the choice freely.

You were foolish. You were glib. You made enemies. You wanted to be a martyr.

You were passionate. You were honest. You made friendships. You wanted to be free.

You are one of the losers. You are part of the problem.

You are part of the solution. You are the answer.

And now you will pay.

Mankind will pay if the world doesn't change.

You know you're in trouble. Don't you? You know this is no idle threat. You sniff the danger. You just don't know the extent of it, yet.

You risked everything. It was worth it.

You don't know the half of it. You never did.

You never doubted the decision.

You are the prey.

You are the answer.

You never understood.

You know enough to keep going.

You don't know what you're saying, that's why you lost. You'll never understand, will you?

You know that enlightenment and freedom do not grow without care, without compassion.

Not until you are dead and buried.

You will not be the last soldier in this war.

Not until there is nothing else to learn.

You are a teacher. You are an artist.

Someone is going to track you down and teach you a lesson.

You will help others see the light.

You will be punished.

You will be freed.

You will be stone dead like your parents, your innocent, loving parents.

You are one of many in a long line.

You deserve worse. You've earned it many times over.

You have made mistakes. You have tried to correct them. And you have tried not to make them again.

You can't hide behind your door, behind your Beardsleys.

You are not hiding. You are connecting, creating.

Victors get revenge. It is one of the spoils.

You will keep fighting until your last breath.

Winners get recognition.

You do not seek recognition. Maybe before, but no more.

Terry is surely one of the winners.

You are one of many.

You are nothing.

You are hope.

You are the enemy.

You are the future.

You are traceable. You have been located.

You are present.

Your name is known. Your street address is on file. Your life has been published and shared and discussed.

You are past.

You are sentenced.

All human beings are born vulnerable.

You have been found.

You will find your way.

An IP address is all that's required.

Any way you can.

You are guilty.

You are human.

You are exposed.

You are naked.

You are a rat hiding in a hole, trembling in the darkness.

You are a tiny white bird flying a flag of artistic freedom across the wide blue sky.

You are dead but do not know it.

You do not fear anything.

You bet everything and lost.

And you would do it all again.

You were never a hero.

You are a human being.

253

You wagered it all just to feel superior, just to feel special.

You changed because it was the only thing to do. You fought because life is creation.

You attacked and demeaned and trolled just to feel better about yourself.

You will fight the good fight.

You deserve what's coming.

You may not get there.

Your borrowed words and your wiki knowledge can't save you now.

Salvation comes in many forms. You never thought it would look like this.

You are on the list.

You are not a name on a roll.

It is a part of your permanent record.

You are not a number.

You will be purged.

You are alive, now.

Excuses don't matter.

Will matters.

Words don't matter.

You define you.

It is too late.

You are eternal. You know who you are.

You are surrounded. You are doomed. Look outside. Look at all those wires, the cables, the towers, the satellite receivers. That is how they will find you.

You will keep going.

But you don't know when.

No one knows when.

But the day will come.

You suppose.

You are a rat in a cage.

You are a freedom fighter, an artist, a creator.

You will be sacrificed for Terry and the others.

You will sacrifice yourself.

You are alone. You are naked. You are defenseless.

You always have been. You finally see it.

You are public. It's the Internet, stupid. Your interwebs lured you into the arena.

You see the end. It is shaped like the beginning.

It was a trap.

A series of traps in the meat of life.

All along.

All wrong. Wrong turns, wrong words. Regrets and misunderstandings surrounded by pale yellow light.

A ruse.

A pretty illusion.

You are exposed, stuck to the fly paper.

You are free. Will.

You lost.

You fade away.

You can't disappear. Not anymore. It is too late.

It is late.

Logging off won't help now.

Logging off won't hurt.

Turning off the lights won't hide you.

You are the light.

Cutting the power and locking the door can't protect you.

The door is locked. You are safe.

You are finished.

You are beginning. Again.

You are dead.

You aren't afraid.

This is the end of you.

This is a new start.

This is the end.

You are resigned. Again.

THE CAVE

At the end of our survey we return to France and the valley of the Vézère. It is only fitting we bring this anthology of anonymity full circle.

Twenty years after the cavern at Lascaux was forever closed to the public, Lascaux II opened. Located a mere two hundred meters from the entrance to the original, Lascaux II is an exact copy—down to the millimeter—of the Great Hall of the Bulls and the Axial Recess. Since 1983 more than two hundred and fifty thousand people per year have lined up to rush through the fake grotto. In 2012 an eight hundred square meter kit reproducing some of the main features of Lascaux opened in Bordeaux and has been traveling the globe ever since. This nomadic representation, this roving cave art circus, is known as Lascaux III.

And in the year 2017 at the bottom of the famous hill beneath its predecessors, Lascaux IV opened its broad shiny doors. Hidden behind glass and gray cement—from the air it looks like a futuristic pigeon spreading big metallic wings—Lascaux IV is a faithful copy of the entire Lascaux subterranean complex, but it is also much, much more.

When you enter Lascaux IV you are handed a tablet computer—the tablet looks to be carved from slate, like something out of the *Flintstones*—to take photos, record information, and create your own art.

Where Lascaux II is incomplete, Lascaux IV is complete, where Lascaux II is passive, Lascaux IV is active. The less hurried tour at Lascaux IV—*a time for contemplation and discovery*, promises the brochure—is followed by a lengthy series of interactive galleries that explore various aspects of Lascaux and cave art. Sections of the cave are suspended from the translucent, airy ceiling. Giant touchscreens hang in floating columns, where visitors can create their own personal exhibition combining modern art and cave art. You, the visitor, become part of the experience. There is a cathedral-like feel to the enormous open spaces. Before you leave the museum, when you return your slate tablet, you are given a code to access a website where you can download everything you saved during your visit. Lascaux IV is a new world, a new multi-level experience. It focuses on interpretation and self-discovery. It plays games with the original.

Lascaux IV has been called an expert forgery, and some say it is better than the real thing. I am tempted to agree. But what is a *real* cave anyway? Wasn't the original Lascaux modified by generations of our forebears? Wasn't it altered for accommodation? Didn't they level the floor? Didn't they bring light into the darkness? Haven't *Homo sapiens* always tried to upgrade our environment? From the very beginning hasn't the human evolutionary journey been one of decathexis, from real to copy to simulacrum?

More than one hundred artists and sculptors

painstakingly fashioned the cave at Lascaux IV. How many worked on Lascaux II and Lascaux III? How many architects, engineers, politicians, managers, truckers, and laborers did it take to recreate and, dare I say, improve upon the original cave? Thousands, surely. But they are all gone now, all forgotten, just like the prehistoric cave painters, just like the Gilgamesh scribes, all consigned by time to anonymity.

And one day we—you and I—will be forever gone, subsumed into oblivion, and all that will remain of our existence will be a name after a name, a painting of a painting, a mention of a memory, a file folder, a cold blue link.

Death is anonymity.

The inevitable fate of every human being is anonymity.

But anonymity is simply a recursion. It is nothing to fear. For anonymity is the true deep state of the universe. All will be forgotten. Anonymity—long before your birth and forever after your death—is the cold eternal flame hidden within the cavern; the illusion is being; the illusion is life. And, sometimes, to relieve us of the often unbearable weight of this mortal illusion, we turn to anonymity. It is a palliative for the temporary burden

We do the best we can. We want to live and we want to be remembered: immortality and identity. So we claw in vain at the illusion hoping to uncover any evidence of our historical existence. We work and we play. With brittle fingernails we dig for truth. We scratch on stones. We stamp clay tablets. We sign parchment and slap at keyboards. And some of us paint pretty little circles in the Anthropocene twilight.

REJECT

Overhead, the smoke detector blinks its one red eye.

You straighten the canvas.

No more mail falls to the floor.

You prepare your paints.

Sunbeams crisscross the room.

You arrange your brushes.

Cracks in the barricades reach for the ceiling.

You stretch one arm after the other as if readying for competition.

There is a stinging rap on the door. Fat, hairy knuckles meeting weak wood.

You ignore the noise.

Then there is quiet.

You don't know what to paint.

There is a painful thump on the door.

You just know you need to create.

And again it is quiet.

You glance at a Beardsley.

Someone rattles the doorknob.

You recount the oriental tulips.

The knocking returns. Loud banging.

You observe a fat pigeon on the skinny sill. It shits white next to a geranium potted in terracotta.

There are no voices, no language. There are no words to be heard.

You inspect the little owl on its shelf.

The door creaks.

The blank space before you widens.

You pick up a brush.

The detector blinks without concern.

You dip the hog bristle toe into a pool of cerulean blue.

The door groans.

Four syllables or three?

The floor shakes.

You don't do that anymore. Forget it.

There is a hollow thud against the door.

Forget words. Forget everything.

The shrieking of splintering wood scares away the incontinent pigeon.

You touch the paint to the coarse canvas.

Deep dark blue bleeds into the unseen fibers, swallowing the white emptiness.

The door disappears.

You turn a line into an arc, an easy bend.

Bootsteps and cursing.

You don't turn. You keep turning.

A violent rush and no breath left.

You are relieved.

The curve is almost a blue circle.

Above, a red light winks.

Terminated.

Larry Francis lives in France with his wife, Maria, and their three children.